SHOWDOWN . . .

All of the onlookers held their breaths as the distance between the two men lessened. It was only Clint Adams who was moving. Dean Teacher was just standing there, waiting for him.

They didn't speak.

There was nothing to say. They both knew why they were there.

The Gunsmith stood easily, his feet spread slightly, watching the other man closely. Sometimes, you could tell by watching a man's eyes when he was going to make his move. Sometimes, you watched his shoulders.

This time, he knew he was going to have to rely on pure instinct.

Sheep, he thought. Damned stupid things for people to be dying over.

Teacher watched Clint Adams closely. The man standing in front of him had a reputation second to none. If he could kill the Gunsmith, then someone would soon be thinking the same thing about him.

He went for his gun . . .

Also in THE GUNSMITH series

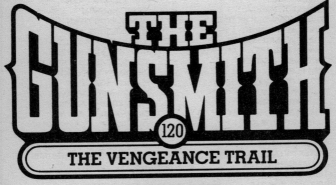

THE GUNSMITH

120

THE VENGEANCE TRAIL

J. R. ROBERTS

JOVE BOOKS, NEW YORK

THE VENGEANCE TRAIL

A Jove Book / published by arrangement with
the author

PRINTING HISTORY
Jove edition / December 1991

ISBN: 0-515-10735-2

Jove Books are published by The Berkley Publishing Group,
200 Madison Avenue, New York, New York 10016.
The name "JOVE" and the "J" logo
are trademarks belonging to Jove Publications, Inc.

PRINTED IN THE UNITED STATES OF AMERICA

10 9 8 7 6 5 4 3 2 1

ONE

When Clint Adams heard the shots he knew that there was only one course of action that made sense for him to take.

Go in the opposite direction.

He also knew he couldn't do that. He just wasn't made that way. No matter how much trouble he got into minding other people's business, he knew he could not turn and ride in the other direction. Not only wasn't he made that way, but his curiosity would never let him forget it. He had to see what was going on.

"Let's go, boys," he said to his team.

He took out his whip and slapped both horses on the rumps. They both jumped, and then took off at what was for them a heady pace. Clint knew that Duke, his big, black gelding, tied loosely to the back of the rig, would think of it only as a pleasant trot.

1

The rig and the team were making plenty of noise but Clint was still able to make out the sounds of the subsequent shots.

He topped a rise and reined the team to a halt. He looked down at the meadow below him and saw that it was dotted with carcasses. From what he could make out, the dead animals were too small to be horses or cows. He finally decided that they were sheep.

There were still a few left standing, but the men with the guns were taking care of that. They fired a few more rounds and about a dozen sheep lay dead.

Now there was only the man.

This was cattle country, and Clint knew how cattlemen felt about sheep, and about sheepherders. He also knew that he was too damned far away to be able to do anything about it. If the three cattlemen wanted to kill the sheep man, there wasn't a whole lot he could do to stop them from where he was.

Unless . . .

Some time back Clint had taken an old .50 caliber Sharps in trade for payment for work he'd done on another gun. He had taken the weapon because he had always been impressed with the piece of history the Sharps had carved out for itself—not this particular Sharps, but the weapon in general.

He reached behind him, into his wagon, and closed his hand over the Sharps. He kept it loaded, but had only fired it once or twice, to make sure it still worked.

He stood up and squinted down into the meadow. He would have only one shot, because the Sharps would have to be reloaded after that, and he had to make the shot count. Maybe if he killed one of the men the other two would panic and run. A killing shot was all he could afford to try. He never even tried to wound a man with his handgun, because that was simply giving the man a chance to fire back. At this distance, that was not a concern, but a one-shot kill was still the only thing that made any sense in this situation—if he was to have any chance at all of saving the other man's life.

Before that could happen, though, he'd have to hit one of them at a range of better than three hundred and fifty yards.

He watched as the three cattlemen beat the sheepherder down to the ground, using not only their hands and feet, but their guns as well. Finally the man was prone on the ground and one of them aimed his gun him.

Clint quickly shouldered the Sharps, sighted on that man, and fired.

Of course, there was no immediate reaction to the shot. He waited the length of time it took the .50 caliber bullet to travel the three hundred and fifty some-odd yards, and then saw the man stagger back as the huge chunk of lead struck him in the chest.

The other two cattlemen looked around them quickly, trying to locate where the shot had come from. They spotted Clint's rig on the top of the rise, and the man standing in it.

Clint began to hurriedly reload the Sharps, but he knew that if the two men were still intent on killing the fallen sheepherder, he'd never be able to load fast enough to kill the both of them. One of them would have to get off a killing shot at the man on the ground.

Instead of firing at the sheep man, however, the two men hurriedly picked up their fallen comrade and ran with him back to their horses. Clint finished loading while they draped the dead man over his saddle and quickly mounted their own animals. Just for effect, Clint fired again, putting one square in the trunk of the tree they had left their horses near.

The men dug their heels into their horses' rumps, and galloped off without looking back.

Clint looked after them, then reloaded the Sharps and replaced it in the wagon.

He sat down, picked up the reins and said to his team, "All right, boys, let's go down and see if we managed to save that man's life."

When Clint reached the man he saw that the beating had been far worse than he'd thought. The man's face was a mass of swelling bruises and oozing cuts. Add the fetal position he was holding himself in indicated that there had to be damage to his ribs, and perhaps more.

Clint leaned over the man and saw that he was barely conscious.

"Where can I take you for help?" Clint asked him. He needed an answer, because the last thing he needed to do was take this man to the wrong place. If he took him someplace that sympathized with the cattlemen, that would certainly do him no good.

"Can you hear me?" Clint said. "Where can I take you to get you some help."

"Lords . . . ," the man muttered, and for a moment Clint thought he was praying before he realized that one of the three towns that were within riding distance from the piece of Wyoming he was standing on was a town called Lords.

"You want me to take you to Lords?"

The man couldn't speak again, but Clint thought he saw a nod.

Lifting him and carrying him to the rig caused the man a lot of pain, but there was nothing Clint could do about that. The man was tall, but he was slender, and Clint had hardly any problem carrying him— except that he had to close his ears to the man's cries of pain. He knew that if he had broken ribs even the slightest movement would cause pain.

"I'm sorry," he told him as he set him down on the floor of the rig as gently as he could, "but considering your condition, I can't afford to go slow. I'll have to move quickly, and you're going to be in a lot of pain."

The man didn't answer, but Clint saw by the look in his eyes that he understood. He huddled on the floor of the rig, holding himself curled up, bleeding from several cuts on his face, and in danger of bleeding even more when some of the swollen lumps split open and bled. Clint was sorry there wasn't more he could do for him personally, but right now all he could do was get him to town, and to a doctor, as quickly as he could.

With that Clint climbed back aboard his rig, turned it around and started for Lords, Wyoming, as quickly as his team would take him.

He hoped that the man would live through the ride.

Dan and Lew Cornell were in a state of shock. They hadn't expected any trouble when they went after Teddy Haslett, as ordered. Now Carl Wilde was dead, and the man who had shot him had been three or four hundred yards away. He probably could have shot them as well, if he'd wanted to. Why he hadn't, they didn't know.

They headed back to the ranch, with Carl Wilde's body in tow, to report to their boss, the foreman of the Double-L Ranch, Sam Pace.

How they were going to explain this neither of them had even stopped to think. All they knew was that they were still alive, and they wanted to stay that way. To do that they had to put as much distance as possible between themselves and that devil with the rifle.

What the hell kind of gun had that been, anyway?

TWO

Clint was so intent on finding a doctor that he barely looked at Lords as a town. He drove his rig down the main street and stopped the first person he saw, a man crossing the street.

"Where's the nearest doctor?"

"Only got one," the man said. Pointing, he added, "Down the street two blocks, and on the right. His office is around the side of the general store. His name's Travis, Doc Travis."

"Thanks."

"You don't look like you need a doctor," the man commented.

"It's not for me," Clint said. "I've got a badly injured man in the back. Thanks again."

"Sure," the man said.

As Clint rode further down the main street, looking for Doc Travis's office, the other man's curiosity got the better of him, and he followed on foot.

• • •

Clint located the doctor's office with no problem. On the front wall of the general store was a small wooden board with Doctor's Office written on it in hand. Clint pulled his team to a halt and dropped down to the ground. He hoped that the man in the back of his rig was still alive.

For a moment, as he looked in at the man, he thought he wasn't, but then he moaned and moved slightly. Clint slid the man out as quickly and as gently as possible, lifted him and carried him up onto the boardwalk, and around the side of the general store to the doctor's office.

The man who had given Clint directions to the doctor's office, and who had then followed him, was named Michael Cooper. Cooper watched as Clint dropped down from his rig and pulled the injured man from the back of the wagon. Cooper immediately recognized the injured man as Teddy Haslett.

"Jesus," he said, "the sheepherder."

He turned and headed the other way on Main Street, his intended destination the office of Tom Lord.

Clint used his foot to knock on the door of the doctor's office, the sound probably unduly loud from inside.

The door swung open and a woman appeared. She was in her early forties, a handsome woman with an impatient look on her face.

"What the hell—" she said, in a decidedly unlady-like manner.

"I'm sorry, miss," Clint said, "but I have a badly injured man, here."

He moved forward, forcing her to back into the office and allow him to pass.

"Where can I put him?" he asked.

"Over here," she said, indicating an examining table.

Clint walked to the table and laid the man on it. As he set him down the man groaned, and blood trickled from his mouth. Clint and the woman's eyes met. The color of the blood made it clear that he wasn't bleeding from the lip, and they both knew what internal bleeding meant.

"Where's the doctor, miss?" he asked. "Dr. Travis? This man needs immediate attention."

"I can see that," the woman said, and leaned over the patient.

"Are you . . ." Clint said.

"Yes," she said, "I'm Dr. Travis. Do you know who this is?"

"No."

"It's Teddy Haslett."

"That doesn't mean anything to me."

"Well, it'll mean something to Tom Lord."

"That name doesn't mean anything, either."

"Well," she said, moving Haslett's head from side to side, "I don't have time to educate you now, Mr. . . ."

"Adams."

"Mr. Adams," she said. She looked at him and

said, "The best thing you could do for all of us right now is to get out of here and let me see what I can do for him."

"All right," he said. "I'll see to my rig and team, and get a room at the hotel."

"Do whatever you have to do," she said, "but get out of my office—now!"

Michael Cooper explained to Tom Lord's secretary that he needed to see Mr. Lord immediately. The lovely, red-haired Miss Harlowe frowned at Cooper who, like almost every other man in town—married or unmarried—tried to find excuses to come up to the office and talk to her.

"This is serious," Cooper said to her. "It's about Teddy Haslett . . . and the sheep."

Kelly Harlowe said, "Wait a moment." She got up and walked to Tom Lord's office door, and Cooper watched her with admiration until she disappeared through her boss's door.

He waited, fidgeting, for several moments, and then she opened the door and said, "You can go in."

He nodded, and she moved out of his way so he could enter.

Tom Lord, the most powerful man in the county, and probably the state, was standing behind his desk, looking at Cooper expectantly.

"This better be important, Cooper," Lord said, "and not some lame excuse to come up and ogle my secretary."

"It is important, Mr. Cooper," Michael Cooper said. "Teddy Haslett is in town."

Lord glared at Cooper and asked, "And what is Haslett doing in my town?"

"He's hurt."

"Hurt?" Tom Lord said, snorting. "He's supposed to be more than hurt."

Michael Cooper stared at Lord, and decided not to ask what that meant.

"Where is he?" Lord asked. "Exactly?"

"At the doc's."

"At the doc's," Lord repeated, a faraway look in his eyes. "Doc Travis."

"Yeah, right, Doc Travis." Where else would he be, Cooper asked himself. There wasn't any other doctor in town, not since Doc Everett died.

"All right," Lord said. "Get out."

"You wanted to know this, right?"

"Yes, Cooper," Lord said. "I wanted to know this. Now get out!"

"Yes sir," Cooper said. He had been hoping for some kind of a reward, but maybe that would come later.

Maybe.

After Cooper left Lord shouted, "Kelly!"

Kelly Harlowe entered his office and waited.

Tom Lord took a moment, as he always did, to look at Kelly. She was twenty-five, tall and slender, except for her big, round breasts. Her skin was white, and peppered with freckles here and there, in some real interesting places. He knew that she had freckles between her full breasts, and she also had some on her sweet buttocks.

Letting Lord play with her freckles was a big part of her job—but she *was* a good secretary.

Tom Lord, at fifty-five, had everything a man could want. He had the biggest ranch in the territory, he had a wife, he had a son and a daughter who were older than Kelly, he owned the town. He had everything he could want—almost.

Some of what he couldn't get from his home was given to him by Kelly Harlowe.

Something no one could give him, however, was to rid the territory of sheep—and to do that, he had to get rid of Haslett.

Which he thought had been taken care of.

"Kelly, get me Sam Pace."

"Yes sir."

"Get him for me now!"

"All right."

"No," Lord said, "you don't understand." Tom Lord was a big man, six-three and—thanks to years of good eating—almost three hundred pounds. He raised a massive fist and brought it down on his desk—hard!

"I want him here . . . yesterday!"

Kelly jumped, blinked, and said, "I'll get him."

"You do that."

When Sam Pace showed up, he was going to have to explain why there was enough of Teddy Haslett for someone to scoop up and take to the doctor—and speaking of explanations, Randi Travis was going to have some explaining to do about why she was even treating him.

When explanations were due Tom Lord, he got them.

THREE

Clint found the livery and made arrangements to have his rig, team, and Duke cared for. After that he went to one of Lord's hotels and checked in. That done, he wondered if he should go and check on the sheep man, Haslett, or go and have something to eat.

He decided to eat.

"You idiots!"

The Cornell brothers flinched as Sam Pace shouted. Pace was the only man they had even seen who was bigger—physically speaking—than Tom Lord. What they didn't know was that that was one of the reasons Lord had hired Pace ten years before. Pace had been foreman of the Double-L for the past six of those ten years.

"Not only didn't you get the job done," Pace said, "but you got Carl killed."

13

"We didn't kill Carl," Dan said.

"That guy with the rifle did," Lew said.

"From four hundred yards out."

"Five," Lew said.

"At least," Dan said.

"That's not possible," Sam Pace said.

"I'm tellin' ya—" Dan Cornell said, but Pace cut him off.

"I'm the one who's got to explain this to the boss, now," he said, "and I'm not taking the blame, do you understand?"

"Sure, boss," Dan said.

"We understand," Lew said.

"Idiots," Sam Pace said. "Take Carl out somewhere and bury him. I'll talk to the two of you later."

Pace watched as the Cornell brothers walked away, leading Carl Wilde's horse. Pace knew that Lord would be sending for him, so he decided to get the jump on his boss and head for town.

Clint found a small restaurant that served a fine steak and good, strong coffee. With his belly full he left the restaurant and headed back to Dr. Travis's office. As he walked toward the office he saw a man ride into town, not quickly, but determinedly. The man rode up to a brick building, dismounted his horse and entered, securing his horse to a hitching post with a flick of his wrist. The end of the reins wrapped itself around the post even as he was going through the front door.

Clint had always wished he could do that.

•   •   •

Sam Pace mounted the steps to the second floor and entered Tom Lord's office. When he spotted Kelly Harlowe seated behind Lord's desk he took a moment to stop and stare at her. He knew she was the boss's property, but there was no harm in looking, was there? She looked up at him and smiled then, and when she smiled at him like that, he wanted to do more than must look—and he had the feeling that she would let him if he tried.

Maybe, one day, he would . . . but not today.

He approached her desk and she said, "He wants you . . . now!"

"I figured that."

"I was sending someone to get you, but—"

"But I'm here," Pace said. He leaned on the desk and, quite by accident—or was it—covered one of her hands with one of his.

"How did you know?" She asked, frowning.

He smiled and said, "I just knew. Can I go in?"

"I think you'd better," she said. "Don't you?" She slid her hand from beneath his . . . slowly.

He stared into her eyes for a moment, then took a deep breath and said, "Yeah, I guess so."

He walked to his boss's door, opened it, and went inside.

Clint knocked on the door to Dr. Travis's office and waited. He didn't knock again, just in case she was busy with her patient. He showed some patience himself, and was amply rewarded when the door opened.

"Mr. Adams."

"Doctor," he said, "how is he?"

She was drying her hands with a white towel, and continued to do so as she stepped back a few steps.

"Come in, please."

He moved past her and she paused long enough to close the door behind him. He could smell the soap on her hands.

"Well?" Clint asked. "Is he all right?"

"For now," she said, "but he's not conscious."

"When will he be?"

She tossed the towel aside and dropped her hands to her side.

"He may never come out of it."

"What do you mean?"

"He has a serious head injury which I can't treat here," she said. "To tell you the truth, I think he'll be dead before the day is out."

"That's too bad," Clint said.

"I did all I could."

"I'm sure you did, Doctor," Clint said. "You don't need to feel any . . . guilt."

She looked at him sharply and said, "I feel no guilt, Mr. Adams. What I feel is sadness, and it's what I always feel when I lose a patient."

"I understand."

She looked away from him, showing him her fine profile, and said, "I'm sorry I spoke so sharply."

"There's no need to apologize. Tell me, does he have any family?"

She looked at him then and said, "Yes, he does. He has a sister, Terry Haslett."

"Where does she live?" he asked. "I'll ride out and tell her."

"I can do that—" she started to say.

"I found him," he said, cutting her off. "If you don't mind, I feel an obligation."

She studied him for a moment, then said, "All right. They have a camp west of town, about three miles. It's where they keep their . . . sheep."

"I suspected that the men who killed him were cattlemen," Clint said. "They killed a dozen of his sheep before starting on him."

"How many were there?"

"Three," he said. "But only two got away."

"You killed one?"

"I wasn't able to do more than that," he said. "I was trying to take their attention away from him, but I guess it was too little too late. They had already done the bulk of their damage."

"Well," she said, "you did what you could. There's no need for you to feel any . . . guilt."

He smiled at her and said, "Touché, Doctor."

He moved toward the door and said, "I'll notify his sister, then. I'm sure she'll be coming in."

"He may not be alive when she does."

"She'll still want to come in to collect the body," he said, opening the door. "Tell me, who would want to do this to him?"

"Pick a cattleman, Mr. Adams," she said. "We have plenty of them."

"Who's the biggest in the area?"

"That would be Tom Lord," Dr. Travis said. "But why blame the biggest?"

"Lord?" he asked. "As in the town name?"

"The same," she said. "He owns most of what you can see from the center of town."

"To answer your question," Clint said, "I'm not blaming the biggest. It was just a question."

He started out the door and she said, "What will you do . . . after you notify his sister, I mean."

He shrugged.

"I'll stay around, I guess . . . for a little while, anyway."

"Then I'll see you around."

"Sure," he said. "See you around . . . Doc."

He left, closing the door gently behind him.

FOUR

"Shut the door!" Tom Lord said.

Pace closed the door and moved further into the room.

Lord was standing, glaring at his ranch foreman.

"What the hell happened?"

"The men were about to finish the job when they were attacked."

"By who?"

"They don't know who he was."

"He?" Lord said. "One man?"

"Uh, yeah, one man."

"And how many of your men were there?"

"Three."

"Three," Lord said, "scared off by one."

"He killed one of my men."

"And what did the others do?"

"They ran."

"From one man?"

"He shot Carl Wilde," Sam Pace said, "from a range of over four hundred yards."

"That's impossible."

"No it's not," Pace said. "There are men who could make a shot like that, with the right weapon."

"Who?"

"Give me enough time I could come up with two or three names, but why would those men be here?"

"Come up with those names," Lord said. "If the sheepherders have hired a gun, I want to know about it."

"They don't have the money for that," Same Pace argued.

"Maybe not," Lord said. "There's a stranger in town. He took Haslett to Doc Travis. I want to know who he is, and I want to know Haslett's condition."

"Should I bring the doctor over here?"

"No," Lord said. "Go and ask her, and let me know. Then find out who the stranger is."

"All right."

"Don't lay a hand on her, Sam," Lord said.

"Don't worry, Tom," Pace said. "I won't."

Pace left, pausing only a moment to exchange glances with Kelly Harlowe.

After Pace left, Kelly Harlowe thought about him. Sam Pace was sort of a younger Tom Lord, as far as she was concerned. She didn't mind warming Lord's extramarital bed when he wanted her to. As far as she was concerned, that was part of her job, what she got paid for. She even thought of herself—sometimes—as a high class whore. That didn't bother her much, because there was a time when she was a low class whore, and being high class was definitely an improvement.

She thought about warming Sam Pace's bed, though, but worried about what Tom Lord would do if he found out. He might kill Sam. Even worse than that, he might fire her. Sam Pace might be great in bed, but he wasn't worth her job.

Not yet, anyway.

Although Sam Pace often referred to his boss by his first name, he never deluded himself that he was considered an equal by Tom Lord. He was Lord's foreman and, even more, his right arm, but he was still just an employee. Pace was happy with that, for now, but things would change soon enough.

Tom Lord didn't think he *had* an equal, anywhere. Sam Pace meant to prove the man wrong.

Lord looked out his window and watched as Sam Pace crossed the street and headed in the direction of Randi Travis's office. Lord had a wife, and he had a mistress, but the woman he'd wanted for the past five years was Dr. Randi Travis—and she would have nothing to do with him. She was the only person who had ever spit in his face—figuratively speaking—and lived.

One day, however, she would come around. He had been telling himself that for the past five years, but he still felt it was true. One day . . .

He only hoped that when that day came, he wouldn't be too damned old to enjoy it.

FIVE

When the knock sounded on the door Dr. Randi Travis thought it was Clint Adams returning again. Maybe there was something he had wanted to say that he hadn't said. He was an interesting man, she thought as she walked to the door, interesting and probably a little foolhardy. Who else would stop to help a sheep man against cattlemen in cattle country?

"Forget something—" she was saying as she swung the door open, but she stopped short when she saw it wasn't him at all.

"Who'd you think I was, Doc?" Sam Pace asked.

"Never mind," she said. "What do you want, Sam?"

Pace was aware of the way his boss felt about the lady doctor. In fact, Sam Pace had had a yen for the good doctor a time or two—like now, when she looked so pretty with a wisp of hair hanging down over her forehead.

"You look like you been working hard, Doc," he said, smiling.

"Is that supposed to be a compliment?"

"When a woman looks as good as you do—" he started, but she cut him off.

"I don't have time for this, Sam. I have a patient who needs my attention."

"That's what I heard," Pace said.

"What did you hear?"

"That a stranger brought that sheep man here for you to look after," Pace said. "That won't sit too well with Mr. Lord, you know."

"I don't care what sits well with Tom Lord, Sam," she said. "You know that, and so does he. Did he send you over here for information?"

"Well, I—"

"You tell him this for me, because pretty soon everyone will know it," she said, cutting off his reply. "Teddy Haslett was badly beaten up and probably won't live out the day. You tell him that."

"He'll be interested to hear that."

"Oh yes, I have no doubt of that," she said. "I can't prove it, but I know it was his men—your men—who did this to Haslett. You tell Tom Lord I hope he's very proud of his men."

"Mr. Lord is always proud of his men, Doc," Sam Pace said. "Tell me something about the man who brought him in. Who was he?"

"A man Tom Lord won't be able to bully or intimidate," Randi Travis said.

"Is that a fact?"

"Yes, it is."

"He must be quite a man, then."

"That doesn't quite follow," she said, "but that happens to be the case, yes. He is quite a man."

"Who is this man, Doc?"

"His name is Clint Adams," Randi said. She had recognized Clint Adams's name, although she didn't let him know that. Now she was throwing the name is Pace's face, and she was oddly satisfied by his reaction. She saw by the look on his face that he also recognized the "Gunsmith's" name when he heard it.

"You've got what you came for, Sam," Randi Travis said. She put her hand against his chest and said, "Now why don't you get out?"

Pace grabbed her wrist in one hand and twisted it, just slightly, enough to hurt.

"Don't be so quick to push me away, Doc," he said, holding on to her wrist. She was in pain, but chose not to show it to him. "I could be the best friend you got, Randi, all you got to do is be nice to me."

"I don't know who I despise more, Sam," she said, "you or your boss, but I'd rather be nice to a rattlesnake than to you or your boss. Now let . . . me . . . go."

She stared into his eyes hard, hoping he would see her resolve there, and not the pain that his grip was causing on her wrist. If he chose to squeeze harder, she knew that the small bones in her wrist would probably break, and that frightened her . . .

"You heard the lady . . ." a man's voice said, surprising both Randi Travis and Sam Pace.

SIX

Clint had reached his hotel when he realized that what he had wanted to do—what he *should* have done—was ask Dr. Travis to have dinner with him. After all, he was a stranger in town, didn't know anyone, and needed guidance to make sure that he didn't get poisoned by bad cooking.

He turned around and walked back to her office. As he came in sight of it he saw a man standing in the doorway, talking to her. He might have turned and walked away then, but their stance indicated to him that she wasn't about to allow him to enter. He watched for a few minutes, and then he saw her put her hand on his chest. It was not a familiar gesture, but one that indicated she wanted him to leave. When he saw the man grab her wrist, he walked down the alley as quietly as he could, until he was almost standing right next to the man.

He heard her say, "...let...me...go," and waited a split second to see if the man would comply. When he didn't, he spoke.

"You heard the lady...," he said.

Sam Pace frowned, then turned his head to the left, maintaining his hold on Dr. Travis's wrist. He saw a man standing about three feet away from him—a tall, slender man whose hands were at his sides, hanging relaxed. Pace, not a gunman, but a man who had known some, recognized the man's relaxed stance, and knew this was a man who knew how to use his gun—and if this was the Gunsmith himself, then he was doubly sure of that.

"Who are you?"

"That doesn't matter as much as you letting the lady's wrist go," Clint said. "Now."

The man stared at Clint a little longer, then looked at Randi Travis and relaxed his hold on her wrist without letting her go. As soon as she felt able to she pulled her wrist free. She wanted to rub it, but didn't want to do it in front of Pace.

"Is your business here finished?" Clint asked.

The man didn't answer.

"Doc?"

"This is Sam Pace, Tom Lord's foreman, and... we have no business," Doc Travis said to Clint.

"That being the case," Clint said, "I suggest you be on your way."

Pace wet his lips, wanting to reply but not knowing what to say. Abruptly, he turned toward Clint and moved past him. As he reached the end of the alley he thought of something to say, but decided that the time to say it was past.

He walked on, his ears burning with embarrassment—which was something the stranger was going to pay for.

"Are you all right?" Clint asked.

Randi rubbed her wrist now and said, "Thanks to you."

"Oh, I don't know," he said. "I get the feeling you could have handled the situation if I hadn't come back."

"Maybe," she said, "maybe not. Why *did* you come back, by the way?"

"It suddenly occurred to me that I was all alone in town, and you were the only person I knew. I wanted to ask you to have dinner with me."

"I don't know if I can—"

"Now it occurs to me that you owe it to me to say yes," he added, smiling to show that he was only half serious.

She studied him for a moment, then said, "You have a point there."

"Then you accept?"

"How could I refuse," she asked, "when you put it that way?"

"What about your patient?"

"I have someone I can bring in to watch him. Shall we say seven o'clock?"

"Seven o'clock is fine," he said. "I'll come by here for you."

"I'll see you then."

She closed the door and for a moment he felt guilty about the way he had manipulated her into accepting his invitation.

But only for a moment.

Pace relayed what had happened to his boss, but he changed the story around a little.

"I braced him, Mr. Lord, but he wouldn't go for it."

Lord, however, was not so foolish that he'd believe Sam Pace had braced Clint Adams, the Gunsmith.

"You braced him, huh?" Lord said. "If you had, Pace, you'd be dead."

"Mr. Lord—"

"More than likely he ran you off."

"Tom—"

"Never mind," Lord said. "You want to salvage your wounded ego with lies, that's up to you, but don't expect me to swallow them. Anyway, you found out what I wanted to know. The damned sheepherders have hired themselves a gunman, and one of the best. You know what that means, don't you?"

"What?"

"I've got to go out and get some gunmen of my own," Lord said. "Some good ones."

"Hungry ones."

"What?"

"You'll need hungry ones," Sam Pace said. "Ones who would face Clint Adams for free, if they had to."

Lord stared at Sam Pace for a few moments and then said, "Sam, sometimes you amaze me."

"What do you mean?"

"I mean half the time I think you may not be as dumb as I think you are."

"Dammit, Tom—"

Lord laughed and said, "Calm down, Sam. Would you be my foreman if I thought you were dumb? Of course not. Now, you get to work and find me some good—and hungry—gunmen."

"What about price?" Sam Pace said.

"You know better than that, Sam," Tom Lord said. "When I want something price is no object."

"Yes, sir," Sam Pace said. "I'll take care of it."

After Sam Pace left, Tom Lord sat back in his expensive leather swivel chair and rubbed his hands together vigorously. He suddenly realized how boring life had become, of late.

It seemed that was about to change.

SEVEN

This time when Clint left Dr. Randi Travis he didn't bother going back to his hotel. He went directly to the livery and told the liveryman that he would saddle Duke himself.

Following Dr. Travis's directions he rode three miles west of town and came upon the sheepherders' camp. It was easy to spot, what with all the sheep that were in the area. He rode past them and the men and women who were tending them and rode to the center of the camp. There was a tent there, and a fire in front of it.

As he approached the tent a man holding a rifle pushed the flap aside, stuck his head inside and said something. A woman appeared and stepped outside, regarding Clint curiously.

"Can we help you with something?"

The smell of coffee was strong in the air and he

33

said, "A cup of that coffee might be nice."

"We don't take to strangers much," the woman said. She was tall, dark-haired, in her thirties, and strongly resembled Teddy Haslett. Clint could tell that, even though the only way he had ever seen Haslett's face was cut, bruised, and swollen.

"I have some news for Terry Haslett, if that's you," he said.

"What kind of news?"

"Are you Terry?"

She hesitated, then said, "I'm Terry."

"I have news about your brother."

The man with the rifle was holding it so that it pointed in Clint's general direction. Now he and Terry Haslett exchanged a quick glance.

"How do I know that you know anything about my brother?" she asked.

"Well," Clint said, "if I had reason to believe my word would be doubted I would have brought along something of his. Unfortunately, I didn't, so I guess you'll just have to take my word for it."

"Why should we?" the man asked harshly, and now he pointed the rifle directly at Clint.

"I'd appreciate it if you'd point that rifle somewhere else," Clint said.

The man stuck his jaw out and continued to point the rifle.

"Do you have some control over him?" Clint asked Terry Haslett.

"When need be," she said.

"Well, have him point that rifle away, or I'll have to take it away from him."

Terry looked from Clint to the man holding the rifle, then back to Clint.

"You think you could do that?"

Clint stared at the woman and said, "Without a doubt . . . but maybe not without killing him first."

The woman matched stares with Clint, then said to the man, "Put up the rifle, Rafe."

"But Terry, we don't know him—"

"If you'd give me half a chance," Clint said to both of them, "I'd introduce myself."

Terry Haslett reached over and pushed the barrel of the man's rifle away.

"Put it up, I said," she repeated. To Clint she said, "Step down and have a cup of coffee, mister . . ."

"Adams," Clint, said, dismounting, "Clint Adams."

"I'll have someone take your horse," she said.

"I won't be staying long," Clint said.

"That's for sure," Rafe said.

"Rafe, take his horse over by ours," Terry Haslett said.

"What?"

"You heard me."

The man pushed his jaw out again, then snatched Clint's reins from his hands.

"Be gentle with him," Clint said, "or he might get the idea you don't like him."

The man squinted at Clint, then walked away, leading Duke.

There was a young girl by the fire and Terry said to her, "Lori, give the man a cup of coffee, and I'll have one, too."

Clint accepted the cup from the girl, who had the

biggest brown eyes he'd ever seen. She appeared to be about sixteen, and would be a full-fledged beauty when she got a few years older.

Clint tasted the coffee and said to the girl, "It's good. Did you make it?"

"Yes."

"It's real good."

"Thank you."

"There was something you wanted to tell me about my brother?" Terry Haslett asked, holding a cup of coffee of her own.

"He's been hurt."

"How bad?" she asked, instantly.

"Pretty bad."

"Damn!" she said. "He's been overdue . . . why didn't you tell me that in the first place?"

"Excuse me," Clint said, "but you people didn't give me much of a chance, did you?"

"No," she said, after a moment. "No, we didn't. We've just become so suspicious of strangers . . . where is he now?"

"He's in town."

"Lords?" she asked.

He nodded.

"He's with the doctor."

Rafe was just coming back and Terry said, "Rafe, saddle my horse."

"Where are you going?"

"Into Lords. Teddy's been hurt."

"We only got his word for that," Rafe said.

"Saddle my damn horse!" she said, demonstrating once again that she was in full and complete charge here. Clint found himself admiring the way she conducted herself.

"I'll go with you—" Rafe started, but she cut him off.

"No you won't."

"Terry—"

"The last thing we need is some kind of show of force in Lords."

"Why the hell did he have to take him *there*?" Rafe demanded.

"That's where he said he wanted to go," Clint said.

"Because he knows Doc Travis is a good doctor," Terry said. She glared at Rafe and said, "Get my horse, and his, too."

Rafe made a disgusted sound and turned to go back to the horses.

"So, he was in shape to talk to you?"

"Not much."

"What happened?"

"Three men beat him up, and killed his sheep."

"He was collecting strays," she said. "We've got to make sure we don't let them wander too far."

"There was about a dozen, and they were all killed by three men."

"Tom Lord's men."

"I couldn't say."

"How did you keep them from killing him?"

"I killed one of them," he said. "The others collected their dead and rode off."

"You killed a man to protect someone you didn't even know?"

"I didn't have to know him," Clint said. "I saw one man being beaten by three, and they were about to kill him. I did what I could to stop it."

Terry Haslett bit her underlip and said, "I appreciate it, Mr. Adams. Don't think I don't."

"I'm sure you do, Miss Haslett," Clint said, as Rafe came walking up leading Duke and a bay mare. "Maybe we'd better get going, if you want to talk to your brother."

She stared at him for a moment. The words, "before he dies," hung in the air unsaid, but she had heard them, all the same.

EIGHT

Tom Lord was looking out the window when Clint Adams and Terry Haslett came riding into town. If he needed any further proof that the Hasletts had hired the Gunsmith, this was it. He watched as they rode past his building and stopped in front of the general store. Obviously, they were going to check on the condition of Terry Haslett's brother, Teddy.

With any luck at all, he was dead by now.

Randi Travis greeted both Clint and Terry Haslett professionally, and admitted them to her office.

"How is my brother, Doctor?" Terry asked, removing her hat. Clint saw that her dark hair had been chopped short by someone who didn't know what they were doing. Maybe she had done it herself.

"He's not doing very well, Miss Haslett," Randi Travis answered.

"Can I see him?"

"He's not conscious," Randi said. "He won't know you're here."

"I'd like to see him, anyway, Doctor."

"Of course, Miss Haslett," Randi said. "Just go through the curtain."

As Terry Haslett disappeared through the curtain Dr. Travis turned to face Clint.

"She seems to be taking it very well," she said.

"She's a strong woman."

"You've only just met her, and already you've formed an opinion?"

"Everyone forms an opinion the minute they meet someone, Doctor," Clint said. "I'm sure you formed one of me when I brought Haslett in."

"And you of me."

"Maybe we should discuss those opinions later on," Clint said, "at dinner."

"Why not?" Randi said. "We'll need something to talk about, won't we?"

"Oh, I don't think we'll have any trouble finding something to talk about, Doctor, do you?"

"Excuse me," Terry Haslett said.

They both turned and saw her standing in front of the curtain.

"While you have been making a dinner date," Terry Haslett said, "my brother has died."

"Was he alive when you first saw him?" Dr. Travis asked. She had already examined Teddy Haslett and found that Terry was right. He had died.

"He was alive when I touched him," Terry said, "and then he died. He—he waited for me."

Terry was sitting down, her hat in her hand. The slump of her shoulders was the only indication of the grief she was feeling.

"Miss Haslett," Randi said, "would you like me to have the body—have him moved to the undertaker's office?"

Terry looked up at the doctor, then stood up, squared her shoulders, and replaced her hat on her head.

"No, Doctor," she said. "I'll be back before dark with a wagon, to pick up my brother's body. We'll bury him out of town. I'm sure none of the towns-people will mind."

Terry started for the door, and Clint was wondering if he should offer to go with her, or just stay out of her way when she turned around again.

"Doctor, please have my bill ready when I come back."

"All right."

She looked at both of them in turn and then said, "I hope you both have a pleasant dinner tonight," and walked out.

"You're right," Randi Travis said.

"About what?"

"She's a strong woman," Randi said. "A very strong woman."

"So are you."

"Yes," she said. "But in a different way."

"I hope what she said won't ruin dinner," Clint said.

She looked at him and smiled.

"No, I don't think it will . . . not if we don't let it."

"All right, then," Clint said, "I'll see you at seven."

He put his hat on and left the office. Outside, he found Terry Haslett waiting by the horses.

"I wanted to thank you again, Mr. Adams," she said. "If you hadn't brought my brother here, and come out to camp for me, he might have died without me having a chance to see him."

"I only wish he could have known you were there, Miss Haslett."

"He knew," she said confidently, and mounted her horse.

"What will you do now?"

"Do? What do you mean?"

"I mean, about your sheep—"

"We'll do what we were going to do before my brother died," she said. "We'll raise them until they're ready for shearing, and we'll continue to fight the cattlemen who are too narrow-minded to realize that there's room here for all of us."

"Like Tom Lord?"

"Especially Tom Lord."

"I wish you luck."

She wheeled her horse around to ride away, then stopped and turned in her saddle to look at him.

"I realize you have a dinner engagement this evening, but I'd like to buy you a drink after I've taken care of my—my brother's body. Would that be possible?"

"I don't see why not," Clint said. "I'll either be at the hotel, or the saloon."

"Which hotel?" she asked. "The Lords House?"

"No," Clint said, "the other one, the, uh—" He couldn't think of the name, at the moment. In fact, he didn't recall seeing a name over the door, or on the building.

"I'll see you later, then."

He watched her as she rode out of town, and wondered when he'd met two such strong, self-sufficient women in the space of a few hours.

Tom Lord watched Terry Haslett ride past his office and out of town, and knew she'd be back soon.

He'd have a reception waiting for her between her camp and town.

"Kelly?" he shouted.

After a moment she appeared and said, "Yes."

"Is Pace still in town?"

"I believe so."

"Get 'im up here!"

NINE

Clint went back to the hotel, dug out some fresh clothes, and had himself a hot bath and a shave. He felt a lot better afterward, and wondered why Dr. Travis had accepted his invitation to dinner when he'd had half of the trail covering him from head to toe, and had probably smelled like a bear.

He'd taken his time bathing, and had gone back to his room after the shave, so by the time he reached the saloon he wondered if Terry Haslett had returned to town to pick up her brother yet. She'd have to bring at least a couple of men with her, and as concerned as she was about a possible show of force, he wondered if that might not cause some trouble.

He walked beyond the first saloon he came to and kept going until he could see the general store. There was no wagon in front of it. He walked further, until he could see the alley where the doctor's office was, and there was no wagon there, either.

He still had a couple of hours before meeting Dr. Travis for dinner, so he decided to take a ride, just to satisfy his curiosity—and the bad feeling he had in his gut.

"Please," Terry Haslett said, "I just want to go into town to pick up my brother's body, that's all."

"Well," Sam Pace said, "Mr. Lord said he doesn't want any of you sheepherders in his town."

"But my brother—"

"Don't beg them, Terry!" Rafe Lewis said.

Terry Haslett was sitting atop the buckboard, holding the horse's reins loosely. Rafe Lewis had been riding on her right, and another man named Henry John was riding on her left. When Sam Pace and four other men appeared in front of them, blocking the road, Terry had spoken urgently to both men.

"Leave your guns alone," she'd said. "That's what they want."

Now she said to Lewis, "Take it easy, Rafe."

Rafe Lewis longed to pull his rifle out and start shooting, but out of respect for Terry he held himself in check.

"Look, Mr. Pace," Terry said, "maybe if I talked with Mr. Lord—"

"There's only one thing Mr. Lord wants to hear from you, lady," Sam Pace said, "and that's that you're leaving and taking your mangy sheep with you."

"I can't do that," she said. "Please, my brother—"

"Your brother's dead," Pace said. "If you want, instead of you going to town to get him, you can wait here while we bring him out to you."

"You would do that?"

"Sure," Pace said, looking at his other men, "all we got to do is tie a rope around the ankles and drag the body out here."

"You sonofa—" Rafe Lewis said. He could take no more, and reached for his rifle.

"No!" Terry Haslett shouted.

Clint heard the shot and knew it had come from close by. It reminded him of hearing the shots that drew him into this mess in the first place, but he could no more ignore it now than he could then.

Besides, this time he felt sure *Terry* Haslett was involved.

"Let's go," he said to Duke, and just a light pressure on the big gelding's ribs sent him off at a gallop.

When Clint spotted them Terry Haslett was still seated on the buckboard, but there was a man lying on the ground. There was a second man on horseback, next to the buckboard. Fanned out in front of her were four men. From this distance, Clint couldn't recognize any of them, but he didn't have to recognize them to run them off.

He drew his gun and fired in the air. The four men turned, and he recognized one of them. It was the man he had rescued Randi Travis from. Now he was doing the same, saving Terry Haslett from the same man.

He fired into the air again, and if the four men had not ridden off, his third shot would have been a lot more precise.

As he reached the buckboard Terry Haslett had stepped down and was leaning over the fallen man.

Clint dismounted and hurried to her side.

"He's dead," she said.

Clint checked the body and found that she was correct. Rafe Lewis was dead.

"You fool, Rafe," she said softly. "You damn fool." She looked at Clint and said, "He went for his gun. He never had a chance."

"What happened here?"

She got to her feet and said, "They were trying to keep us from going to town for my brother's body. I tried to keep Rafe from doing something . . . fool-ish . . . but you can see I wasn't able to."

"Who's this fella?" Clint asked, indicating the other man who was still on horseback.

"That's Henry John," she said, looking at the other man. "He's with us."

"Well, Henry John, step down and help me—" Clint started, but Terry cut him off.

"He can't hear you," she said. "He's deaf."

"Deaf?" Clint said, looking at the man. Actually, he was hardly a man—or, depending on how you looked at things, almost a man. He looked to be about eighteen or so.

"Been that way since he was born."

"Can you get him to help me lift Lewis into the buckboard?"

"Yes," she said. "Yes, I can."

"When that's done," Clint went on, "I'll ride into town with you so you can pick up your brother's body."

"Once again I'm in your debt."

She wondered how much longer she'd feel that way if the bodies kept piling up, and he continued to be on hand.

"After that we can talk to the sheriff."

"A lot of good that will do," she said doubtfully.

"What do you mean?"

"Wait until you meet the sheriff."

TEN

When they reached town Clint suggested that he go and see the sheriff while Terry Haslett and Henry went to the doctor's office to pick up the body of Teddy Haslett.

"Meet me over there," Clint said, "and we'll see if we can't get something done."

"I doubt it," Terry said.

"There's no harm in trying," Clint said. Terry just shrugged. She was a strong woman, but how much could she take. She looked dangerously close to just caving in and not caring about anything anymore.

Clint rode over to the sheriff's office, dismounted, and left Duke loosely tied to a hitching post. He walked to the door, knocked, and entered.

The office looked much like any other sheriff's office. A desk, a rifle rack, a potbellied stove with a coffeepot on it. The man behind the desk, however, did not look like any other sheriff Clint had ever known. Even seated, Clint could see that the man was well over six feet. He wore a shirt that had the sleeves removed, so as to accommodate biceps that looked like stone. His chin also looked as if it had been chiseled from rock.

"Sheriff?"

Clint had to ask because there was no star on the man's chest.

"That's right," the man said in a deep bass voice. "Sheriff Will Haywood. What can I do for you, stranger?"

"I brought a man into town earlier today, name of Teddy Haslett."

"The sheep man," Haywood said. "Doc Travis already told me he's dead. Small loss."

"I beg your pardon?"

"This is cattle country, mister. Sheep ain't wanted here."

"Does that mean that sheep men can be murdered with no fear of reprisals by the law?"

"Huh?"

"Cattlemen can get away with killing sheep men?"

"Far as I'm concerned they can," Haywood said. "Any sheep man comes around here is looking to get killed."

"That's crazy," Clint said. "You're the law."

The man regarded Clint coldly from beneath heavy black eyebrows and said, "Best you remember that, mister . . ."

"Adams," Clint said. "Clint Adams."

He watched the sheriff's face for any trace of recognition, but the man's ignorance seemed to extend that far as well. He had no idea who Clint was.

"Look, Sheriff," Clint said, "Terry Haslett is going to come over here in a little while to file a complaint."

"Against who?"

"Some cattlemen who killed one of her men."

"Another dead sheep man?" Haywood asked, raising his eyebrows. "Sounds like it was a good day."

"Are you an elected official, Sheriff?" Clint asked, and then realized what a foolish question that was. This was cattle country, and a cattle town.

"That I am, Mr. Adams," Haywood said, "and damned proud of it."

"I see. And I suppose Mr. Lord was a big supporter of your campaign?"

"Mr. Lord is a good citizen and he knew what was good for this town."

"And that was you as sheriff?"

"That's right." Haywood said. He stood up, as if his size would add weight to what he said next. "You got a problem with that?"

For a moment Clint considered telling the man who he was, thus pitting his reputation against the man's size, but he thought better of it.

"I do, yes," he said, "but there doesn't seem to be much I can do about it."

"No, there ain't," Haywood said. "Let me give you some advice. If you're gonna be staying in town for a spell, don't be showing no sympathy for the sheep people. You'll wear out your welcome here real soon."

"I can believe it," Clint said.

"Anything else I can do for you, mister?"

"No," Clint said, "not at the moment, Sheriff. You've done quite enough."

Haywood nodded, and remained standing until Clint left the office. For all Clint knew, after he left, the man might have remained standing, impressed as he apparently was with his own size.

Outside Clint stepped down from the boardwalk, retrieved Duke's reins, and started walking toward the doctor's office. He felt obliged to let Terry know that she had been on the money in her opinion of the sheriff. There didn't seem to be much law for sheepherders in Lord's Texas.

Still, murder was murder, and the law was the law, wasn't it? All they had to do was go outside the town to let some federal law know what was going on in Lords, and get a federal marshal in here to do something about it.

ELEVEN

When he reached the doctor's office Terry and Henry already had Teddy Haslett's body in the buckboard with that of Rafe Lewis.

"Terry . . ."

"You don't have to tell me," Terry said. "I warned you."

"Yes, you did," Clint said, "but you don't have to stand for this."

"Oh, no?" she asked. "And just what is it I can do about it?"

"You can telegraph for a federal marshal."

"On Tom Lord's telegraph?"

She had a point. If Lords owned the town, or a good portion of it, then it followed that he also owned the telegraph office.

"Then send a rider to the next town and use the telegraph there."

"The next town with a telegraph is two days' ride from here," Terry said. "A lot can happen in two days."

"So what are you going to do, then? Give up?"

She didn't look Clint in the eye.

"I haven't decided what I'm going to do," she said. "All I want to do now is bury my brother, and Rafe."

She caught Henry's attention and motioned that they were leaving. He nodded, and mounted his horse. Lewis's horse was tied to the rear of the buckboard.

Terry started to climb aboard the buckboard and Clint stepped in and helped her.

"I thank you for your help, Clint," she said, "and your concern."

"I'd like to come out and see how you're doing," he said. "Maybe tomorrow."

"If you like."

"I'd like to find out what you decide to do."

"Come ahead, then," she said indifferently.

He watched as she drove the buckboard out of town, unaware that Tom Lord was also watching from his window.

Lord watched the buckboard leave town, and then turned to face Sam Pace.

"You're a disappointment to me, Sam," he said. "You've backed down from Clint Adams twice."

"He's the Gunsmith, Tom," Pace said. "You pay me a lot, but not enough to get killed."

"Have we confirmed whether or not he's actually working for them?"

"What do you think? He's been there twice in one

day when we had them where we wanted them. You think he's doing that out of the goodness of his heart?"

Lord turned and looked out the window thoughtfully.

"No," he said. "A man with his reputation wouldn't be doing that, would he?"

"You're damn right he wouldn't."

Lord turned and looked at Pace.

"Aren't you the one who told me those sheepherders didn't have enough money to hire a gun like his?" he asked his foreman.

"Maybe Terry Haslett is paying him off in some other way," Pace suggested.

Lord thought that one over. No denying the woman was attractive, but was she enough payment for a man like the Gunsmith—and was she the type to use herself that way?

"You come up with anybody for me, yet?"

"A couple of possibilities," Pace said. "I'm still working on it."

"Until we get someone, and until they get here," Lord said, "I want everyone to steer clear of those sheepherders. Understand?"

"Why?"

"Maybe we'll lull them into a false sense of security," Lord said. "Maybe when we strike, we'll take them by surprise. And maybe," he said, looking out the window again, "maybe after these two deaths, they'll just up and move on by themselves."

"Terry Haslett doesn't strike me as the type of woman to give up," Pace said.

"I'll keep your opinion in mind, Pace," Lord said. "I also want everyone to stay clear of the Gunsmith."

"I don't think that will be a problem."

"Good, then that's all."

"Yes sir."

"Oh, Sam," Lord said, as Sam Pace moved toward the door.

"Yeah?"

"I want the Cornell brothers fired."

"What?"

"And the men you had with you today, the ones who ran from Adams. I want them fired, too."

"That's five men, Tom—"

"Replace them," Lord said. "That's your job, isn't it?"

There was an implied threat in the way Tom Lord said "your job" so Pace just nodded and said, "Yes, sir, that it is."

TWELVE

It had been a fairly full day for a man whose intention was to just pass through—or even by—Lords, Wyoming, and Clint was looking forward to a leisurely dinner with Dr. Randi Travis.

He knocked on the door to her office at the agreed upon time and was pleasantly surprised when she answered. She was wearing a dress, which fit her very nicely, showing off a trim waist and full breasts. Her hair, which had been pinned here and there with wisps escaping, was now hanging down to her shoulders. She smelled clean and fresh from a bath, with very little perfume.

"Wow," he said.

"I'll take that as a compliment."

"It is," he said. "You look wonderful."

"Thank you," she said. "I don't really get the opportunity to wear dresses much."

"You should wear them more often."

"All right," she said, "we can stop with the compliments now."

"Why?"

"They make me uncomfortable," she said, as they walked. "I don't know how to react to them—unless they involve my work, that is . . . and I don't get too much of that."

"Why not?" he asked. "You appear to me to be a fine doctor."

"It's still very hard for most of the townspeople to accept a woman doctor," she said. "The longtime town doctor died some time ago and I've been all they've had, ever since. Oh, they come to me when they or their kids are sick, but that's the reason— because I'm all they've got."

"Maybe all it will take is a little time," he said.

"Maybe," she said. "Lord knows, I've got enough of it to spend."

"Do you know a good place to eat?" he asked, changing the subject.

"What kind of food do you like?"

"I'm a simple man," he said.

"Meat and potatoes."

"Sounds like heaven to me."

"I know just the place."

She took him to a small café run by a husband and wife. Clint had been to many places in many towns, and they usually served good food because the people involved were concerned not only with making a living, but with serving food that people could actually eat and enjoy.

The couple—Chuck and Tisha—also seemed to be very friendly with Dr. Travis.

"I delivered Tisha's baby a couple of years ago," Randi told him as Tisha brought them their coffee. "A beautiful baby girl."

"That's not all of it," Tisha said. She was a pretty blond with the clearest blue eyes Clint had ever seen. "The baby was in danger the whole time, and Dr. Travis saved her."

"She was turned around," Randi said, "and the cord was around her neck."

"I don't know how she did it," Tisha said, "and I was no help. She has magic hands. I'll be right back with your dinner."

"She seems fairly impressed with you as a doctor," Clint said.

"I saved her child's life, even before she was born," Randi said. "That tends to instill . . . respect."

"And friendship?"

"Definitely," Randi said. "Tisha and CJ—he likes to be called CJ—are two of my best friends in town."

CJ, tall, slender, fair-haired, and good-looking, came out during their meal to make sure they were satisfied, and they assured him that they were. The steaks were cooked to perfection, and the coffee was definitely to Clint's liking, strong and black.

As they left, Randi hugged both Tisha and CJ, and Clint shook their hands and assured them that this was the best meal he'd had in months.

"Why isn't their restaurant busier?" Clint asked. "The food is great."

"Tom Lord."

Clint was hoping to get through the night without hearing Lord's name again, but that was probably too much to hope for.

"How did they run afoul of him?"

"They refused to sell him a piece of their business. Their place used to be very busy, but Tom Lord passed the word on them, and now very few people eat there—mostly strangers passing through."

"Well, I'll make sure to have my meals there while I'm here."

"And how long will that be?" she asked.

"I don't know."

"How involved are you going to get with Terry Haslett?" Randi asked.

"How do you mean?"

"Well, I don't mean . . . personally," Randi said. "I mean, now that she's lost her brother she might lose everything. Do you intend to help her?"

"If she wants my help."

"Are you going to wait for her to ask?"

"Why?"

"You don't strike me as that kind of man."

"What kind is that?"

"The kind who waits for people to ask for his help, and then charges them."

"I'm not," he said. "I don't hire my gun out, if that's what you mean."

"Well, that was part of it," she said. "I certainly didn't mean to insult you, but you do have a reputation."

"I'm aware of that."

"Even if it's not all earned."

"It's not that it isn't earned," he said. "It's just that most of it isn't real."

"Well, what I really meant was, you didn't wait for an invitation when you went to Teddy Haslett's aid, and you helped Terry later on. She told me about Lord's men trying to keep her from picking up her brother's body. The man is just . . . monstrous!"

"Do you know him well?"

"I know him well," she said, "but not as well as he would like."

"Ah . . ."

"What's that mean?"

"It means you have better taste in men than to, uh, get to know him better."

"I sure do. I'd never let him near me, and not only because he's married."

"You mean he's not a devoted husband?"

"Ha! Just ask his secretary—on second thought, don't go near Kelly."

"Kelly?"

"Kelly Harlowe," Randi Travis said, not without some heat, "has the tongues of half the men in this town dragging on the ground whenever she walks by."

"Is she that attractive?"

Randi almost answered quickly, but stopped, considered, and then said, "I guess to be perfectly honest the answer is yes. She has red hair," Randi added, as if that explained everything.

"Well," Clint said, "I *was* thinking about going up to see Lord. I guess I couldn't very well avoid her doing that, could I?"

"Why would you go to see Lord?"

"Like you said," he answered, "I don't wait to be asked for help. I'll go talk to him on Terry's behalf."

"There's a danger in that, you know."

"I know," he said. "He'll think they've hired me, but he must think that already. By going up to see him I'll also dispel that rumor before it gets around."

They had reached her office and stopped by the door.

"I have a room behind the office," she said. "It's modest, but it's a place to sleep."

"Uh-huh."

They stood there awkwardly for a moment, and then he leaned over and kissed her. She didn't react immediately, but then she kissed him back, their bodies not touching. It was a very pleasant kiss, although not as ardent as he might have liked. She kept her lips together, although she did soften them quite a bit. He thought a moment about trying to slip his tongue past her lips, but decided against it. As it turned out, it was a good decision. She was not quite ready to go that far, let alone further still.

"I'd invite you in, Clint," she said, placing her hand on his chest gently, "but . . . it would be a little quick for me."

"I understand, Randi," Clint said. "Thanks for having dinner with me. I appreciated the company."

"Thank you for asking me," she said. "I enjoyed it. Good night."

"Good night."

After she went inside he realized how early it was and headed for the saloon.

Poker would have to replace the other pleasure he'd had in mind.

THIRTEEN

When Clint entered the saloon his first thought was whether or not Tom Lord owned it. He decided it was unlikely. He had deliberately chosen this place, which had a simple sign over the door that said Saloon, over the fancier Steer Palace across the street. If Tom Lord owned a saloon in this town, it would be the Steer Palace.

Clint hadn't seen the inside of the Steer Palace, but he could guess what it looked like. Green felt tables scattered around the room, crystal hanging from the ceiling, maybe even a small stage where scantily dressed girls danced, and then moved out into the crowd to . . . mingle.

This place was a cowpoke's saloon. Bare wooden floors and tables, one faro table in the corner, no stage, two bored-looking girls working the room, wearing low-cut dresses, showing the tops of their creamy breasts but not much more. Men came here to drink, and to play poker with other men, and not with a professional dealer.

Clint walked to the bar and asked for a beer.

"Comin' up," the bartender said. His sleeves were rolled up, revealing strong forearms; he wore no tie and there were stains on the front of his shirt. He'd have been fired from the Steer Palace in a minute.

"There ya go," the said. "Two bits."

Clint dropped the money on the bar and took two swallows of the cold beer.

"Correct me if I'm wrong," he said to the man.

"Go ahead."

"This place is not owned by Tom Lord."

"Ha!" the bartender laughed. "Lord would sneeze on this place. Naw, he owns the Steer Palace, across the street. You want loose women and crooked dealers, go over there."

The man seemed to suddenly realize what he'd said, and looked around to see if anyone had heard him. Luckily, he and Clint were alone at the bar, and there were only two or three inhabited tables in the place.

"Don't worry," Clint said, trying to soothe the man's fears. "He won't hear it from me."

The man grinned sheepishly and said, "Every once in a while it just sorta slips out, ya know?"

"I know," Clint said. "Does this place get busier?"

"You're passin' through, ain't ya?"

"Might be."

"Well, this is about it, mister. We don't offer half what they offer across the street."

"As long as I can get a cold beer, and maybe a poker game."

"Cold beer I got," the man said. "You'll have to scout up the game yourself."

"Any players in here now?"

"Corner table, Slim Young likes to play. He can't hardly afford to play across the street. Might be one or two others. Wouldn't be a big game."

"I'm just looking to pass the time," Clint said.

"If you want, I'll ask for ya."

"I'd appreciate it."

"Sure."

The bartender came out from behind the bar, talked to Slim Young and a couple of others, all of whom agreed to play.

Clint threw the bartender a tip and sat down with three men.

"You'd get a more interestin' game across the street," Slim Young said.

"I don't feel like watching a professional dealer at work tonight," Clint said, shuffling the fresh deck the bartender had given him. "Draw and stud all right with you fellas?"

They all agreed, and Clint dealt out a hand of five card stud.

Slim Young got an ace and Clint said, "Bet it."

"Two bits," Young said daringly, and tossed the money in to the center of the table.

Dan and Lew Cornell were standing across the street in front of the Steer Palace when Clint Adams walked into the saloon across the street. They had been drinking at the Palace, which they knew was owned by their exboss, Tom Lord.

"He thinks he's so high and mighty," Dan had said at one point, "firing us like that."

"Yeah," Lew said, "like he was God or somethin'." And then Lew started laughing at his own joke and said, "Get it? God, and 'Lord'?"

"It ain't that funny, Lew," Dan said.

They were standing at the bar. Seated at a table across the room were the other three men who had gotten fired. They were likewise drinking and grousing about being let go.

"What we should do, you know," Dan said to his brother, "is burn this place down."

"Let's do 'er," Lew said. "Let's go outside and see where's the best place to start the fire."

So they had walked outside and as they did they saw Clint Adams across the street.

"Wait a minute," Dan said.

"For what?"

"There's the sonofabitch what got us fired," Dan said, pointing.

"That's Clint Adams," Lew said, squinting in order to see through the alcoholic haze. "That's the sonofabitch what got us fired."

"Right," Dan said. "And if it wasn't for him, we wouldn't be fired."

Drunkenly, Lew stared at his brother, and then said, "You know, you're right."

"We ought to burn *him*," Dan said, "not the damn saloon."

"You're right again," Lew said, then he frowned

and asked, "Danny? Can we take the Gunsmith, just the two of us?"

"Maybe not," Dan Cornell said, rubbing his jaw thoughtfully—the exaggerated thoughtfulness of a man who is drunk, but does not know it. "But there's three other men who got fired because of him."

"Hey, that's right!" Lew said, his face brightening—then he frowned. "So?"

"And together, the five of us can take him. After all, he's just one man, right?"

"Right!"

"Come on," Dan said. "The others are inside." And they went back into the Palace to present their plan to the rest.

FOURTEEN

After playing poker for an hour Clint was ahead twelve dollars. The others were not very good players, but one of them—a man named Kennedy—had gotten very lucky. A bad player, he stayed in when he shouldn't have, and twice had filled a belly straight. If Kennedy had been an experienced player, Clint would have folded both times, but it took an hour to get all of the players straight in his mind. The other two—Slim Young and a man named Dade— were bad players, and they had no nerve. At least Kennedy had nerve enough to try for the straights.

After an hour and a half, Clint had doubled his winnings. At that point he almost felt bad about taking their money—almost. He was dealing when the batwing doors opened and Terry Haslett walked in. He started to rise, but she waved him off, motioning for him to finish his game, and walked to the bar. She stood at the bar like a man, ordered a beer, and drank it like a man. The saloon was half full, though, and none of the men in it *thought* she was a man—not the way she filled out her jeans. They must have also known who she was, though, because no one approached her.

Clint finished dealing a hand of five card stud, and when he looked at his cards he saw that he had dealt himself four of a kind—queens. Slim opened, the other two called, and then he raised. Slim and Kennedy called, while Dade dropped out.

"Cards," Clint said.

"Two," Slim said.

Kennedy said, "Three."

Clint dealt them their cards, and then said, "I'll play these." Sitting on what was virtually an unbeatable hand, he hoped that at least one of them had improved their hand to some extent.

"I'm gonna bet a dollar," Slim said, "into a pat hand." He had a smirk on his face. He had drawn two cards, which meant he could have made four of a kind from three of a kind. Kings or aces, that's what he needed to beat Clint's queens.

"I'm out," Kennedy said, throwing down his cards.

Clint was about to raise, wishing he'd gotten this hand in a high stakes game instead of a penny-ante game, when the batwing doors opened again, and five men walked in. Clint didn't recognize any of them, but it was plain they were looking for him. Once they were inside and had spotted him, they fanned out, facing him in a semicircle.

"Take a walk, boys," Clint said to the other players.

"What?" Slim said. "Come on, Adams. Play cards!"

Kennedy and Dade looked up and saw the five men facing Clint.

"Slim," Kennedy said. "Slim!"

"What?"

Slim looked up at Kennedy, then at the five men.

"Shit," Slim said, pushing his chair back. He placed his cards facedown on the table carefully before he got up and moved away, followed by Kennedy and Dade. Clint could hear chairs scraping the floor as the rest of the people in the saloon started moving for cover. Some of them slipped behind the five men and out the door.

At the bar Terry said something to the bartender, who nodded.

Clint set his cards down easily, then sat back in his chair. His right hand hung down over the arm of the chair. If he was going to draw he was going to have to do it from beneath the chair's arm. He'd have preferred a chair with no arms, but there were none in the saloon.

"Can I help you boys?"

The man in the center did the talking.

"You got us fired, Adams."

"How did I do that?"

"You killed one of our men," the man said. "A friend of ours."

Now Clint knew who they were—at least, two of them.

"Let me guess," he said. "Two of you beat up Teddy Haslett earlier today. He died, you know. I think the law would like to see you."

"You killed our friend," the man said again.

"A pretty good shot it was, too, don't you think?"

"Shit," another man said, "I never seen a shot—"

"Shut up, Lew!" the center man said. Lew was standing just to his right, and they looked enough alike to be brothers.

"And you other three," Clint said. "Let me guess again. You were with Sam Pace this evening when I ran you all off. Who pulled the trigger then?"

No one answered.

"Well, no matter," Clint said. "I think I'll just take the five of you over to the jail. We'll let the law decide who did what."

The man in the center laughed.

"There's five of us, Adams."

"What's your name?" Clint asked.

The man hesitated, then said, "Dan Cornell."

"Well, Dan, it may surprise you, but I can count. I know there are five of you."

"You're a dead man, Mr. Gunsmith."

The air in the room seemed to perk up, and men brought their heads out from under tables when they heard the name Gunsmith.

"You and your friends look drunk to me, Dan," Clint said.

"We ain't drunk."

"If you weren't," Clint said, "you wouldn't be willing to die over a job. There are other jobs."

"Nobody pays like Tom Lord."

"So you'll die for a well-paying job," Clint said. "How many of you want to die?"

A couple of the men exchanged anxious glances,

looking as if they had bought into the game and were having second thoughts.

"Decide now," Clint said.

At least two of them might have backed down right there and then if Dan Cornell hadn't gone for his gun.

Clint kicked the table over in front of him and drew his gun. His first shot hit Dan Cornell in the chest before the man could clear leather, and his second killed Lew Cornell, who died with a confused look on his face.

A shotgun blast sounded from the direction of the bar, and two of the remaining men spun away and fell to the floor. Clint shot the fifth man as he was turning, probably to flee out the door, but by that time it was too late. Clint had to finish the move, and the man fell to the floor, dead.

Clint stood up and walked over to the five men, examining them and making sure they were dead. Only then did he look over at the bar. Terry Haslett was standing there, a shotgun in her hand. Undoubtedly, she had gotten it from the bartender. It was a Greener, all bartenders' favorite.

Clint stepped over the bodies, dropping empty shells to the floor and loading new ones into his gun. He had it holstered by the time he was standing next to Terry.

"You're pretty handy with that," he said.

She handed it back to the bartender and said, "It's pretty hard to miss with a shotgun."

In the room others moved away from the walls and out from under tables to look at the dead men themselves. For many of them this would be something they could talk about for a long time.

"You recognize these men?"

"Yes," she said. "Like you said, three of them were with Sam Pace earlier, when they killed Rafe."

"Who pulled the trigger on Rafe?"

"Sam Pace," she said. She looked at the dead men with distaste and said, "I wish he was lying there right alongside of them."

"It could still happen," Clint said. He looked at the bartender and said, "Two beers." He was picking his up when the batwing doors opened and admitted the sheriff, all six-seven of him. He had a gun in his hand, and it looked like a toy. Clint could see now that the man kept his badge pinned to his belt, which was why he hadn't seen it on the man's chest in his office.

"What the hell happened here?" he asked.

"You ought to carry a rifle, Sheriff," Clint said. "A pistol in your hand is kind of hard for anyone to take seriously."

FIFTEEN

Of course, the last thing Clint expected after the shooting in the saloon was that Terry Haslett would end up in his bed, but here she was, seated astride him, her head thrown back, her large firm breasts in his hands as she rode him up and down, moaning and crying out. . . .

Sheriff Haywood wanted to take Clint in—and Terry—but the bartender and Slim Young backed Clint's story to the hilt.

"Them fellers came lookin' for him, Sheriff," Slim Young said. "He didn't have no choice—and the little lady jest helped him out."

Haywood looked at Clint and Terry, both of whom regarded him without expression.

"Listen, Sheriff," Clint said. "You have nothing to

worry about. These men don't even work for Tom Lord anymore."

"What?" the sheriff said.

"That's right, Sheriff," the bartender said. "I heard them say they got fired. That's why they were after Mr. Adams. Said he was to blame for them getting fired."

"How's that?" the sheriff asked, and Clint knew the man would be sorry he asked.

He told the sheriff that two of them had killed Teddy Haslett, and that the other three had been present when Sam Pace killed Rafe Lewis.

"Are you going to go and get him now, Sheriff?" she asked.

"Get who?" the sheriff asked, warily.

"Sam Pace."

"Why would I want to do that, little lady?"

"You just heard—"

"Anybody else see him killed this man besides you?"

"Well, yes, my man, Henry John."

"This Henry John," the sheriff asked, "will he make a statement?"

"He can't," she said. "He's deaf and dumb."

"Then it's just your word against Sam Pace's, ain't it?"

"That's right, Sheriff," Terry said. "Just the word of a sheepherder against a cattleman's." Angrily, she stalked out of the saloon.

"You got any more questions, Sheriff?" Clint asked.

"No, but—"

"Sorry I can't help you clean up," Clint said, and hurried after Terry.

He'd caught up to Terry on the boardwalk outside. She had been standing there, her shoulders hunched, hugging herself.

"Go ahead and cry," he told her.

She looked up at him then and said, "Not here, not where everyone can see." She turned to him then and said, "Take me somewhere I can cry, Clint?"

So he'd taken her to his room.

When they got to the room, though, crying seemed to be the last thing she wanted to do. She turned into him as soon as they entered and was in his arms, kissing him. He held her tightly and returned the kiss with enthusiasm, and then undressed her.

They fell on the bed together. She started kissing his chest, licking his nipples, reaching between them to take hold of his rock hard penis. He kissed her breasts, sliding a hand down between her legs at the same time and finding her wet. He knew she'd be wet. He was able to smell it while undressing her.

"Please," she said in his ear, "now . . ."

She didn't want any kind of foreplay, this girl, she just wanted to go, and he was only to happy to oblige her. . . .

Staring up at her now he squeezed her nipples between his fingers as she continued to bounce up and down on him. Maybe, he thought, she couldn't cry. Maybe this was what she needed to release the emotions that were being pent up inside of her. Maybe she wasn't in bed with him, maybe she was in bed with any man.

And maybe he shouldn't be examining this so closely. He was in bed with a healthy, attractive, and eager woman, and when was the last time he took the time to study on a situation like this?

He pulled her down to him enough so that he could reach her breasts with his mouth and tongue. He suckled them while they continued to move their hips in unison, and when he felt her begin to tremble he pulled her to him, crushing her breasts against his chest, and they came together, shuddering, groaning, groping . . . and only then did she start to cry. . . .

Afterward, she apologized.

"Don't," he said.

She sat up in bed and hugged her knees. He admired the strong line of her back.

"But I don't—this wasn't me—I . . ."

He sat up and put his hand on her shoulders. Involuntarily, she flinched.

"What are you apologizing for?" he asked. "The sex? Or the crying?"

She shrugged and said, "Both, I guess."

"Terry—"

She tossed the sheet aside abruptly and swung her feet to the ground.

"I have to go, Clint."

Ordinarily, Clint enjoyed watching a woman dress, but Terry Haslett did it so frantically there was no enjoyment in it. She was in a frenzy to finish and get out the door.

She stopped at the door and stammered, "Clint, I . . . I . . . oh, I'm sorry . . ." and she ran out.

Clint knew she was going through a lot, and he hoped that she would be able to cope with it all and make decisions that were right for her.

SIXTEEN

Tom Lord woke and ran his hand over Kelly Harlowe's sweet ass. She was lying next to him in his suite in the Lords Hotel. He had long since told his wife that when he worked late he would spend the night in his suite. Whether or not she knew what he really did in that suite did not concern him. She liked being Mrs. Thomas Lord too much to risk objecting.

Kelly had a light sprinkling of freckles on her back which he liked, and he leaned over to lick them, kneading her ass at the same time.

"Mmmm," she moaned, and wiggled her ass.

Tom Lord was as hard as a raging bull. He got on his knees behind her, lifted her ass up and took hold of her hips. He rammed himself home and she cried out and began to bang her ass into him.

Kelly Harlowe was a godsend. When he had found her two years ago, working in his Steer Palace, he had taken her to bed immediately. Prior to that taking a woman to bed had been a hit or miss proposition with him. He could no longer perform with his wife, and occasionally he was able to with Sara, the young, black maid his wife had insisted she needed—the girl had small, firm breasts, but she had nipples like grapes. With Kelly Harlowe, however, there had been no question—and he had never failed to perform with her in two years. On the rare mornings when he woke up beside her, he usually had a pulsing, demanding erection—like today.

Lord went from raging bull to wounded bull, as he bellowed like one when he exploded inside of her. He withdrew from her and flopped down onto his back. She kissed his neck and snuggled into the crook of his arm, and they fell asleep again . . .

When morning came Clint took some time before rising to think over the events of the day before. It hardly seemed possible that all of that could have happened in one day, but it had. Eight men had died, and he'd killed—or contributed to the killing of—six of them. It was the other two deaths, however, that concerned him more.

It irked him that a man like Tom Lord could get away with having two men murdered. There had to be some way of getting some federal law in here to take some action. Unfortunately, the only way he could see meant he had to leave town, and his leaving town might leave Terry very vulnerable. With her brother and one of her men gone, how long would it be before she lost some of her other men?

Would young Henry John be able to keep her safe? Not very likely.

He sat up in bed and wondered when Terry Haslett's life had become his responsibility.

He rose, washed with the basin and pitcher the hotel provided, then dressed. After breakfast he'd go and talk to Tom Lord, and see what good that could do. After all, he only had other people's opinions about what kind of man Lord was.

It was time for him to form his own.

The second time Tom Lord woke he told Kelly to have breakfast sent up for him, and then to go and open the office. Kelly dressed quickly and left the room. She went downstairs and told the clerk what to have sent to Lord's room, and then went back to her own room to bathe. She wanted to wash Lord's smell off of her before she went to work.

Thankfully, she thought as she bathed, the man only slept in town two or three days a month. Other times he would take her right in his office, but those times were becoming fewer and fewer, as well. Maybe the time was near when he'd just pay her for her skills as his secretary—not that she really had any, but after two years she prided herself on the fact that she ran his office pretty well.

Usually, she opened the office at ten and he would come lounging in around twelve. Today, since he'd slept in town, maybe he'd come in at eleven. She'd have coffee ready for him, in either case, and then he'd lock himself in his office for a while, and she'd be able to take some time to breathe and think. What she thought about was saving enough money to leave Lords and go to San Francisco. That time was still at least a year away, but there was always the chance that the right man would come along . . . oh, not to marry, but someone to whom she could hitch her wagon—at least as far as San Francisco . . .

Clint went back to CJ and Tisha's restaurant and had breakfast there. They treated him just as well as they had the night before, when he'd been there with Randi. There were no other diners in the place. He told them both how much he'd enjoyed breakfast, and they told him to come back for lunch.

When Clint entered Tom Lord's office he knew immediately that the woman behind the desk was Kelly Harlowe. Randi Travis had been right, the woman had red hair—but she had much more than that. For one thing, her face was arresting, beautiful actually, with an unusual mouth, wide and thin-lipped, yet moist-looking and inviting. When she looked up at him and smiled, he saw that her mouth was just slightly crooked beneath a nose that was just a touch too long. She had green eyes too. A woman with green eyes could be forgiven a lot, but this one had nothing to be forgiven for. Put the mouth and nose and eyes together, and her face looked just right for her.

"Can I help you?" she asked, looking him up and down with interest.

"I'm looking for Mr. Lord."

"I'm sorry, but he's not in right now."

"When do you expect him?"

"Not for at least an hour or so, I'm afraid," she said. "Is there something I could help you with, mister . . ."

"Adams, Clint Adams."

"Oh, yes . . ." she said, and looked at him with even more interest.

"You know who I am?"

"Oh, yes," she said again. "I've heard of you, and I'm sure Mr. Lord will want to speak with you."

"In an hour?" he asked, looking past her at the closed door of her master's office.

"At least that," she said. "I'm being quite truthful, you know. He really isn't in."

"I believe you."

"Good," she said. "I wouldn't want us to start out on the wrong foot."

He perched a hip on her desk and said, "Tell me something?"

"What?"

"What do you think of your boss?"

She took a moment to think and when she spoke she did so with an enigmatic smile on her face.

"He pays very well."

"You know," he said, "just last night I had five men tell me the same thing."

"Really? Do they work for him?"

"They did," he said, standing up, "but they're dead now."

Her smile faded and she said, "Really?"

"Really," he said. "I'm telling the truth. After all, we wouldn't want to get off on the wrong foot, would we?"

SEVENTEEN

When Tom Lord came into his office Kelly couldn't wait to tell him who had been there for him. She wanted to see the look on his face.

"Who?" he asked.

"Clint Adams."

"When was he here?"

"About forty minutes ago."

"What did he say?"

"Just that he wanted to talk with you."

"And what did you tell him?"

"That you weren't in."

"Did you tell him when I would be in?"

"No," she lied. "But I have the feeling that he'll be back."

"All right," he said, and headed for his office.

"He said something about killing five men last night," she called after him.

He stopped, and then turned to look at her.

"What?"

She repeated it.

"Who?"

"I don't know," she said. "But he said they used to work for you."

"If he killed five men last night," he asked, "why isn't he in jail?"

"I guess you'd have to ask the sheriff that."

"I will," he said. "Get him up here."

"I have work—"

"Now, Kelly," he said. "Go and get him."

"Yes sir."

When she left he couldn't see the satisfied smile on her face.

Tom Lord went into his office, closing the door behind him. He walked directly to his window and looked down at the street, watching Kelly hurry down to the sheriff's office. What he didn't see was the man standing in the doorway across the street, watching his window . . .

Clint watched Kelly Harlowe leave the building and couldn't help admiring her. She was tall and slender, with long legs, but she was also full-breasted. He could see why the men in town lusted after her.

He looked up at Lord's window then and saw the man standing there. He had also watched as the man entered the building a few moments earlier. He had never seen Tom Lord before, but the man had walked with a self-important swagger, and it wasn't hard to guess who he was.

Now that he knew Lord was there—and alone—he stepped out of the doorway and started across the street as Lord turned away from his window.

When the knock sounded on his door Tom Lord naturally thought it was Sheriff Haywood.

"Come on in, Sheriff," he called out, "and you'd better have a good explanation as to why Clint Adams isn't in jail this morning."

"If I was in jail," Clint said, "I wouldn't be able to be here, now would I?"

Lord looked up from his desk quickly, and Clint knew why the man was a success. In a split second Lord resigned himself to the fact that Clint was there, and managed to size him up, as well.

"Clint Adams," Tom Lord said. "This is a pleasure."

"Is it?" Clint asked. He moved further into the room, positioning himself directly in front of Lord's desk. "A moment ago you wanted me in jail."

"Did I?" Tom Lord asked. "If I did, it's only because I heard you killed some of my men last night."

"They used to be your men, Mr. Lord. Seems they got fired, and they held me responsible."

"Now, why would they do that?"

"Whatever reasons they had, they tried to make me pay. I had no choice but to defend myself."

"I see," Lord said. "Then I guess there's really no reason for you to go to jail, is there?"

"I guess not."

"And are there any reasons for you to stay in town, Mr. Adams?"

"Well, maybe one or two."

"Such as."

"I like it," Clint said. "It's a nice town."

"And we'd like to keep it that way," Lord said. "If you stay around, there's liable to be more trouble."

"Is that a threat of some kind?"

"Why, no, why would I want to threaten you?" Lord asked innocently. "Fact of the matter is, a man with your reputation attracts trouble, and I think this town would be better off without you in it."

"Why don't we stop fencing with words, Mr. Lord?" Clint suggested. "I have the feeling you're a little bit better at it than I am."

Tom Lord studied Clint for a few moments, then said, "All right," and sat down behind his desk. "How much?"

EIGHTEEN

"How much?" Clint repeated. "I don't understand. How much for what?"

"I thought you wanted to stop fencing," Lord said. "How much do you want to leave town."

"I don't want your money, Mr. Lord."

"You don't?" Lord asked. "Well then, what's Terry Haslett paying you?"

"She's not paying me anything."

They both heard the door open outside. Clint turned and saw that Kelly Harlowe had returned, and seated herself behind her desk.

When he turned back to Lord, the man had a different look on his face.

"Maybe the Haslett woman is paying you in some way I can't," he said. "Miss Harlowe out there, though, that's a different story. I'll bet she can more than match anything Terry Haslett is giving you."

"I'll tell you what, Lord," Clint said. "All you have to do is leave Terry Haslett alone, and I'll leave."

"If that's the case," Lord said, "it's done."

"Her . . . and her sheep."

At the mention of the word *sheep* Tom Lord's face darkened.

"Dammit, Adams, you know that sheep and cattle don't mix. Her sheep could infect every head of cattle on this range—and most of them happen to be mine."

"That doesn't have to happen, Lord," Clint said. "She's willing to keep her sheep away from your cattle—"

"But she wants to water them, right? That's the same thing."

"You know, Lord," Clint said, "I've never really understood the stubbornness of a cattleman. You have an unreasoning fear of things you don't understand. First barbed wire, and now sheep—"

Lord stopped him by slamming a huge hand down on his desk.

Sheriff Haywood, who had obviously entered when Kelly Harlowe did, stepped into the room.

"Can I do something for you, Mr. Lord?"

"Yes!" Lord shouted. "Get out!"

"But . . . but you wanted to see me—"

"Get out and wait outside!" Lord shouted. "And close my damned door."

"Yessir," Haywood said. He backed out and pulled the door shut behind him.

"Look, Adams," Lord said, "this is just going to lead to bloodshed."

"Blood's already been shed, Lord," Clint said. "Your men killed Teddy Haslett, remember?"

"I had nothing to do with that. Besides, those men were fired, and you killed them last night. What more do you want?"

"A man named Lewis was also killed, by Sam Pace. You going to fire him, too?"

"If it'll get you to leave, yes."

"And then rehire him the minute I'm gone. You know, Lord, I think this town needs some help from outside, some federal help—"

Lord started laughing, and Clint stopped talking.

"Are you threatening me, Adams?"

"Well, I thought I was, yeah . . ."

"Mister, I got more pull in the state capital than you could imagine. You want to send some federal law in here, you go right ahead."

Clint frowned. He knew Lord was probably telling the truth.

"Well then, I only see one way to make sure that Terry Haslett and her sheep are safe."

"Move them out."

"No," Clint said. "I'll just have to go out and camp right alongside them."

"You do that, Adams," Lord said. "I know your reputation, all right, but I also know that you're only one man. If those sheepherders scraped up enough money to hire themselves a gun, I can hire a dozen—two dozen! What will you do then?"

Clint stared across the desk at Tom Lord. That was a very good question. If Lord sent a dozen—or two dozen—guns against him, what the hell could he do?

Feeling he'd finally gotten the upper hand he was looking for, Lord sat forward and folded his hands on his desk.

"Adams, I think you've only got one course of action here."

"What's that?"

"Convince the lady to take her sheep elsewhere."

"Where?"

"I don't care where," Lord said, "but off my range, and away from my cattle. Understand?"

"I understand," Clint said. "Now you understand something. Before I let you hurt that woman, I'll come after you and kill you . . . and I'll come right through as many guns as you can send against me. That's a promise."

Clint turned, walked across the room, opened the door and stepped out. Kelly Harlowe looked up at him and Sheriff Haywood looked over at him from across the room.

"He's ready for you now, Sheriff," Clint said.

Haywood frowned, then hurried past Clint into Tom Lord's office.

"Get off on the wrong foot with the boss?" Kelly asked.

"Both feet, I'm afraid."

"Well," she said, resting her chin in her hands, "I hope that doesn't mean we can't be friends?"

"I'll keep it in mind," Clint said. "Good day, Miss Harlowe."

"Kelly."

"Kelly," he said, and left.

"What did you want me for, Mr. Lord?" Sheriff Haywood asked.

Tom Lord's back was to the lawman, but he could see the big man's reflection in the glass of his window. He looked down and saw Clint Adams leave the building and cross the street.

"Never mind," he said.

"What? I thought—"

"Get out, Haywood," Lord said. "Get out and go to my ranch and tell Sam Pace I want to see him."

"I can't leave town," Haywood said. "I'm the law—"

"You want to stay the law in this town, Haywood? Or you want to go back to being the smithy?"

Haywood waited half a beat and then said, "I'll tell Pace you want him."

"You do that."

As Haywood left the room Lord thought about Clint Adams's parting words. Knowing the reputation—and the legend—of the Gunsmith, Lord wasn't about to disregard the man's threat.

Sam Pace had better come up with some pretty damned good guns.

NINETEEN

When Pace got to Tom Lord's office he gave his boss a list of names that he had come up with.

"How many of these men do you think will be available?" Lord asked.

"For what you can pay?" Pace asked. "All of them."

"Good," Lord said. "Get them."

"How many?"

"Like you said," Lord said. "All of them."

"All of them?"

"Every last one—and tell them to bring their friends."

Sam Pace sent out a dozen telegrams that morning, and instructed that any replies be brought to Tom Lord's office immediately.

"Yessir, Mr. Pace," the clerk said. "Directly to Mr. Lord's office."

"Give them to his secretary."

The mousy, bespectacled clerk's eyes lit up and he said, "Oh yes, to Miss Harlowe. Yes indeed, Mr. Pace. I'll take care of it personally."

Pace smirked, and left the office. He had left his horse out front, and he mounted it now and headed back to the ranch. Lord hadn't been out there in a couple of days, and he hadn't spent a full day on the ranch in weeks.

Somebody had to run it.

Olivia Lord believed she was a handsome woman.

Sitting in front of the mirror, regarding herself critically, she knew she could not compete with someone like her husband's secretary, Kelly Harlowe, but at forty-seven she was still a handsome figure of a woman. Her breasts, for years high and firm, were not as high and firm as they once were, but she knew she'd never have trouble getting a man into her bed. There were plenty of hands on the ranch who would have come running if she crooked her finger at them. She didn't have to do that, though. She had *one* man to replace her husband in her bed, and he did that quite nicely. Truth be told, Tom had not been able to satisfy her for quite a few years, but this man didn't have that problem.

She'd been very glad that her husband had not returned home last night. She knew that he had probably spent the night in bed with Miss Harlowe, but that didn't bother her. As soon as it became apparent that he wasn't returning home, her new man had slipped right into bed with her, and it had been quite a night.

She heard a horse out front and walked to the window of her bedroom that overlooked the front of the house. Hurriedly, she finished dressing and went downstairs. As she arrived there the maid, Sara, was letting the foreman, Sam Pace, in.

"Miz Lord is—" Sara was saying, but Olivia cut her off.

"I'm here, Sara," she said. "Let Mr. Pace in."

"Ya'll can come in," Sara said, and stepped back.

"That'll be all, Sara," Olivia said. "Go back to what you were doing."

"Yes'm."

Both Pace and Olivia waited until Sara was out of sight, and then she melted into his arms. Their mouths locked in a hungry kiss, and one would not have guessed that they had spent the entire night together. They kissed like a man and woman who had been separated for months.

"Is he coming home tonight?" she asked breathlessly.

"I doubt it," Pace said. "There's a lot going on, and I think he'll want to stay in town."

"Oh, darling, good," she said, and they kissed again.

Olivia had always known that Sam Pace wanted her, but it had only been a few weeks ago that she had given him the opportunity to make her happy—and he had.

"He's worried about the Gunsmith, and he's had me send for some extra guns."

"My God," she said, "wouldn't it be wonderful if this Gunsmith killed Tom?"

"Or if *someone* killed him," Pace said, "and the Gunsmith got the blame."

"I'd have everything, then," she said.

He held her more tightly and said, "And I'd have you."

"Yes, you would, my darling," she said, her mouth pressed to his. "You would, you would . . ."

Even as her tongue slid into his mouth Sam Pace couldn't help thinking that once he had her, it would be *he* who actually had everything . . . everything that he had ever wanted!

He slid his hands down to cup her middle-aged ass and kissed the silly, foolish woman as hard as he could.

Joe Lang had seen Sam Pace enter the main house, and he knew what was going on in there, even if no one else did. Lang was sixty, and wasn't a wrangler anymore. He was a ranch hand, but he had worked for Tom Lord for thirty years.

Someone ought to tell the boss what was going on between his wife and his foreman.

Yep, someone should. . . .

TWENTY

Clint walked to CJ and Tisha's restaurant and put away two pots of their fine coffee while he thought the situation over. He was about to order a third pot when the door opened and another customer stepped in.

"Well, good afternoon," Randi Travis said.

"Doctor," Clint said, greeting her. "An early lunch?"

"Late breakfast, is more like it," she said. "I was called out early this morning, and I'm only just getting back."

"Emergency?"

"Oh, Thad Bennett broke his leg—Thad is fourteen, and he was helping his father with the chores—but you don't want to hear about that."

"Is the boy all right?"

"Of course he is," she said. "He had me for a doctor, didn't he?"

Clint slapped himself in the forehead with the heel of his hand and said, "Stupid me!"

Tisha came out and greeted Randi, and took her order for eggs.

"I'll bring another pot of coffee," the pretty blonde said, and went back to the kitchen.

"What have you been doing?" Randi asked.

"Thinking."

"About me, I hope."

"Some," Clint said. Randi's mood was a bit more flirtatious than it had been the day before. Was she sorry she had sent him away last night? He was. He would much rather have woken up with her this morning than with Terry Haslett.

"Mostly, about sheep and cattle."

"Oh, that. Any new developments?"

"I guess you could say that."

He was telling her about what had happened the night before when the eggs and coffee came, and then told her about his visit to Tom Lord.

"Clint," she said, when he was finished, "aren't you taking on just a little bit more than you should?"

"Maybe," he said, "but I'm sort of locked into this thing now."

"Why? Because of Terry?"

"More because of her brother, and of Rafe Lewis. I'd hate to see her end up that way, wouldn't you?"

"Well, of course I don't want to see her killed—but would they do that?"

"Do what?"

"Kill a woman?"

"Randi," Clint said, "if Tom Lord brings in outside guns, there are men who would kill her just for the practice."

Randi shuddered.

"Maybe Tom Lord was right."

"About what?"

"Maybe you should leave—don't misunderstand me," she added, hurriedly. "I don't want to see you leave, but if you weren't here there would be no reason for him to bring in those kind of men."

"You know what's wrong with that logic?"

"What?"

"It's totally correct."

"Before you commit yourself anymore," she said, "why don't you go and find out what Terry wants to do ?"

"I'll do that," Clint said, "as soon as I finish sharing this pot of coffee with you."

"You can go now," she said, "and share dinner with me later."

"Is that an invitation?"

"It is."

"Then I accept."

"Good. Same time?"

"Same time," he said, standing, "if I'm still here."

She sobered and said, "Well, if you're going to leave, make sure you come by and say good-bye."

"I'll see you tonight," Clint said, "no matter what happens."

He left money on the table for the coffee and the food, and left to go to the livery to saddle Duke.

• • •

During the ride out to the sheeperders' camp Randi Travis's logic echoed in his head. If he left, Lord wouldn't bring in the extra guns, but if Clint left the man wouldn't *need* any extra guns to do what he wanted to do. He'd be able to drive Terry and her people away with the men that he had on hand.

Still, Randi Travis was a very smart woman. There was no point in his making a decision until he found out what Terry Haslett wanted to do.

As he approached the camp Terry Haslett came out of the tent and waited for him. By her side was Henry John, holding a rifle.

"Hello, Terry," Clint said.

She didn't answer him right away. In fact, she seemed to be having some trouble looking him directly in the eye. He assumed that she still felt that the time they'd spent together last night had been a mistake. He was sorry for that.

"Hello, Clint," she finally said.

"Does he know how to use that gun?" he asked. He was looking at Henry John when he asked, and the boy's face remained impassive. There is a tendency when dealing with deaf people to wonder if they are really deaf. That's because people who aren't deaf have a hard time understanding how someone who is deaf can function.

"He can fire it," she said. "I doubt he can hit what he aims at."

Henry John, unable to hear what was being said,

simply continued to stare at Clint.

At the fire crouched a different young girl from the one Clint had seen the last time he was there. She was tending to a coffeepot, and something else that was cooking.

He looked around, but all he saw were sheep. No other people.

"Where are all the others, Terry?" he asked.

Now she finally dragged her eyes up to look at him when she answered.

"They're gone," she said. "They're all gone. There's just Henry John, Margarite . . . and me."

Under the watchful eyes of Henry John, Clint dismounted, saying, "We have a lot to talk about."

TWENTY-ONE

Clint sat around the fire with Terry and Margarite. Henry John went to look after the sheep. He took his rifle with him.

Margarite handed Clint a cup of coffee.

"Thank you, Margarite."

"You're welcome."

Those were the first words he had heard her speak, and it was only then that he was sure that she could talk, and was not deaf like Henry John.

"Margarite is Henry John's sister," Terry explained.

"I see."

"Why are you here, Clint?"

"I talked with Tom Lord this morning."

"And?"

"He thinks you should take your sheep and leave."

"That's what every cattleman thinks, everywhere we've been, and everywhere we might go."

"Then you're staying?"

"I don't know what else to do," she said. "If I leave, then Teddy died for nothing. Yes," she said, looking him in the eye, "I'm staying."

"Can you tend your sheep, just the three of you?"

"We can manage," she said. "It's not the sheep we would need help with."

"I know," he said. "It's Lord and his men. Terry, I can help you, but first you have to know what could happen."

"What?"

He explained about his conversation with Lord, and even threw in what Randi had said.

"Do you understand this?" he asked. "If I stay, I could be bringing you even worse trouble."

She studied him for a moment, and then said, "What could be worse, Clint? If you're asking me if I want your help, the answer is yes. Now I guess the final decision is yours."

"There's no decision to make, Terry," he said. "I can't let you face Lord, Pace, and their men alone. I'll have to stay out here with you, though. Is that all right?"

"Sure," she said. "Maybe we'll even teach you to be a shepherd."

"Yeah," he said, "why not, and I'll teach Henry John how to shoot. Sounds like a fair exchange to me."

He handed Margarite the empty cup and stood up.

"I'll have to go back to town to get my things—my team, my rig. I'll bring everything out here."

As he turned to leave she stood up quickly and put her hand on his arm.

"Whatever happens," she said, "I'll always be grateful."

He put his hand over hers, and she eased hers from beneath his, as if his touch made her uncomfortable.

"I'll be back soon," he promised.

Before leaving town for the sheepherders' camp Clint felt he owed Randi an explanation about why he wouldn't be around for a while. He drove his rig from the livery and stopped at her office.

From his window Tom Lord saw Clint Adams driving his rig down the main street, and he frowned. Could it be that the man was leaving town? Had their conversation convinced him that he had no chance against Tom Lord?

Lord would have liked to believe that, but somehow he doubted it.

If Clint Adams was, indeed, leaving town—and the county—all well and good, but Lord chose to think that he'd be seeing Adams again, and soon.

He also chose to believe that if and when he did see Adams again, it would not be good news for the man known as the Gunsmith.

Clint knocked on the door of Randi's office and was admitted.

"It's early for dinner, isn't it?" she asked.

"Dinner is what I came to talk about," Clint said. "I can't make it."

"Ah," she said, nodding. "You went out to the camp and spoke to Terry?"

"Yes," he said. "Most of her people have been scared off. She's out there with a deaf-mute boy, and a young girl."

"So you're going to go out and stay with her?"

"I'm going to stay with them, and help them," Clint said.

"How do you get yourself into these things?" Randi asked.

"I've often wondered that myself, believe me," Clint said. "I just seem to have a knack for finding people who need help."

"Did you ever think that maybe you have a need to find people who need help?"

"Whoa," Clint said. "I think that's a little too deep for me to start thinking about at this stage of my life, Doctor."

"This is a hopeless situation, Clint," she said. "Tom Lord will send so many guns against you that—"

He held up his hand and she stopped.

"I know all of this, Randi," he said. "I've told myself this many times already."

"And you're still going out there?"

"The fact of the matter is," he said, "they have a better chance with me than without me."

"And you have a better chance with them than without them . . . of getting yourself killed!"

"I was hoping you'd understand," he said, spreading his hands helplessly.

She folded her arms over her breasts and said, "Well, I'm sorry, but I don't understand death wishes."

Clint hesitated, then said, "Well, I guess there's nothing left to say, then."

"I guess not."

Clint opened the door and, with regret, left. She was an impressive lady, and he would have liked to get to know her better.

TWENTY-TWO

The next seven days were uneventful.

When Clint first joined Terry at the camp he asked her how long they needed before she was ready to do what she had to do with her sheep. She said she had a buyer coming in two weeks' time.

"That's why we can't leave."

"Did you ever tell Tom Lord that?"

"Yes."

"What did he say."

"That he didn't want sheep buyers here anymore than he wanted sheepherders, or sheep."

"How many sheep do you have?"

"We had a thousand," she said. "I'll have to do a count to see how many we've lost."

"Well, I saw a dozen dead that first day."

"We've lost more than that, both to Lord's men and to natural causes."

"Natural causes?"

"Some of them have starved to death—the weaker ones. Others have died of thirst."

"What have you been doing for water?"

"Teddy was taking the buckboard and getting buckets of water. We dug a trench, and we were trying to keep it filled for them to drink from."

"Did it work?"

"For some. The weaker ones were never able to get to the water. The strong always got there first."

Just like humanity, Clint thought.

Several days later Clint went out with Terry to take a head count. It was decided—or rather, dictated by him—that she would never go anywhere without him, and that Henry John and his rifle would stay with Margarite. Clint didn't think the other two would be targets for trouble. Terry was the one he wanted to keep safe.

While they counted he asked her what the buyers used the sheep for.

"Mostly the wool," she said. "Especially back East—and they also slaughter them for the meat, after they're shorn."

"Shorn?"

"After the wool is shaved off."

Clint had never tasted lamb. He asked her what it was like.

"It's not like beef. Lamb has to be cooked well— and when it is cooked well enough, it's very tender and tasty. In fact, that's what was in Margarite's stew last night."

Clint hadn't realized that he'd been eating lamb.

In fact, he hadn't even asked what it was, he had just eaten it—and enjoyed it.

"You don't kill them yourself for the meat, do you?" he asked.

"No," she said. "But when one dies, we don't let the meat go to waste."

Their count came up nine hundred and twenty, meaning that they had lost eighty for one reason or another.

"We can live with that," she said later, "but not much more."

The first couple of days he was there Clint had given Henry John instructions on the proper way to fire the rifle. It had been difficult in the beginning, but Clint quickly learned that being deaf did not make Henry John stupid. In fact, the young man was quite bright, and was a good student.

The mystery to him remained the young girl, Margarite. Although she was not deaf and mute, she spoke very little to him or, he noticed, to Terry. She also managed to communicate very well with her brother without speaking, but he supposed they'd had a lifetime to perfect their ways of communicating with each other. Watching them do so fascinated him.

At the end of the first week they were having breakfast around the fire, the four of them.

"Clint, what do you think is going on?" Terry asked.

"What do you mean?"

"I mean nothing's been happening," she said. "We

haven't even seen the slightest sign of Lord's men, and believe me that's unusual. What do you think they're planning?"

He put his empty plate down and poured himself another cup of coffee.

"First of all," he said, "I'm sure they're trying to put us off our guard."

"You mean they want us to relax?"

"Yes."

"Ha! Not much chance of that."

"I also think that Tom Lord is waiting for some more men."

"What kind of men do you mean? Gunmen?"

"Well, he had to replace the five men he fired, but yeah, I'm sure he's bringing on some men just for their guns."

"To send against you?"

He nodded.

"I'm also sure he feels justified in doing this," he added. "After all, as far as he's concerned, you hired a gun first."

"But we're not even paying you."

"You'd never convince him of that," Clint said. "Tom Lord can't conceive of someone doing something for nothing. It's not something he could understand."

"To tell you the truth," Terry said, "it's not really something I can understand, either." She waited a beat and then said, "Why *are* you helping me?"

He did not relish going through the same scene now that he had gone through with Randi a week ago.

"I'm not sure," Clint said. "Maybe I think you need me."

"I do," she said, "but I still don't understand what's in it for you? It certainly isn't . . . me."

They had taken care of that question days ago . . .

For the first few days Terry had been extremely jumpy around Clint, until he finally broached the subject one night over the fire, while Margarite and Henry John were off tending the sheep.

"Terry, I hope you know that I'm not waiting to get you into my bed again."

"What?" she asked, looking up at him, somewhat shocked. The flames flickered in her eyes as she stared at him, wondering if she had heard him right.

"You've been uncomfortable around me ever since I got here. I can understand how you feel about . . . that night, but there's no reason to be nervous about it. It's over, and it was a mistake. I'd like us to be able to get past it. All right?"

"I'm sorry . . ." she said.

"There's no reason to be sorry," he said. "Let's just be friends . . . okay?"

He put his hand out to her, and she just smiled and took it.

"Okay."

"Look," Clint said, "let's not waste time trying to figure out what I'm doing here—I'm here."

"Who's uncomfortable now?" she teased him.

He laughed with her and said, "I just don't like to spend a lot of time examining my own motives. You need help, and I'm helping you."

"At considerable risk to yourself."

"I'm aware of that, but then life itself is a considerable risk, isn't it?"

"I'm aware of *that*," Terry said.

"Come on," Clint said, "have another cup of coffee and we'll go out and relieve Margarite and Henry John."

TWENTY-THREE

Kelly Harlowe was not in a very good mood.

For the third day in a row she had been awakened by Tom Lord's roving hands. She was on her knees now with Lord taking her from behind, moaning out loud because she knew he liked to hear her. Suddenly, Lord didn't seem all that concerned about going home at the end of the workday, and Kelly had had to put up with him at night, and in the morning. She didn't think the old bull had it in him anymore, but apparently she brought it *out* in him.

Lucky her.

She closed her eyes now and tried to imagine that it was someone else pounding in and out of her. At first she conjured up the image of Sam Pace, but his face was quickly replaced by that of Clint Adams. She knew that Adams had left town, but she also knew from hearing Lord talk with his men that

Adams was staying out at the sheepherders' camp.

She squeezed her eyes shut tightly and imagined that it was Clint Adams she was in bed with. . . .

Sam Pace slid his cock into Olivia Lord and she shuddered and wrapped her meaty thighs around him. His face was buried in the crook of her neck, so she couldn't see the bored look on his face. He slid his hands beneath her, cupped her large buttocks, and began to thrust into her as hard as he could. She liked it hard and fast, which was fine with him. The sooner he got it over with, the sooner he could go and get some breakfast and get to town.

Of late, Tom Lord had not made a point of coming home at night—either that, or he *was* making a point of *not* coming home at night. Considering where he was spending those nights—and who with—Pace couldn't really blame him. If he had a choice he'd rather be in bed with Kelly Harlowe than with Olivia Lord, any day.

Olivia began to groan and writhe beneath him, so he knew they'd be done soon.

Today was the day Pace expected some of the hired guns to arrive in town, and he wanted to be there to meet them. He wanted to make it plain to them right off who they were working for. Sure, he'd be paying them with Tom Lord's money, but he wanted these men to feel that they were working for him.

One of them was going to be picked for a very special job, one that would make all the hours he had spent in bed with Tom Lord's cow of a wife worth it.

Olivia Lord began to bellow *like* a cow as she approached her climax, and Sam Pace closed his eyes tightly, increased the speed of his thrusts and, thinking about Kelly Harlowe, managed to finish with her. . . .

Doctor Randi Travis was angry with herself. She was thinking quite a bit about Clint Adams, a man she had dinner with once, a man who hadn't been around in a week. When she should have been working she was thinking about him, and about what her friend Tisha had said to her at breakfast. . . .

"You've been in a very bad mood of late," Tisha had said.

"What do you mean?"

"I mean since Clint Adams left town you aren't fit to be around. You finally find a man you want, Randi?"

"That's ridiculous!" Randi said.

"Wanting a man isn't *ridiculous.*"

"I barely know him."

"So, get to know him."

"He's not even here."

"He's out at the sheepherders' camp, isn't he?"

"So?"

"So go out and see him," Tisha said. "You can use a ride and some fresh air."

"That's crazy," she said. "He's out there with Terry Haslett."

"Is there anything between them, do you think?" Tisha asked.

"Yes," Randi said. "They've both got a death wish."

"Come on, Randi—"

"I will not chase after a man . . ." Randi said, letting the rest of the sentence trail off.

"You'll never catch a man," Tisha said wisely, "by not chasing him."

"I've got work to do," Randi said.

"Take a day off, Randi," Tisha called after her as she left. "Go and see him!"

"Dammit!" Randi Travis said.

She left her office, locked it, and walked to the livery to rent a horse.

As Sam Pace was riding into town he saw Randi Travis riding toward him. Here was a woman in her forties who hadn't succumbed to a spreading ass and sagging tits, he thought. This woman looks the way Olivia Lord *thinks* she looks.

"Going for a ride, Doctor?"

"None of your business," Randi snapped.

"Maybe you'd like some company," he called after her, but she ignored him and rode on.

He laughed shortly and directed his horse toward the livery. The stage would be arriving soon, and there should be at least four of the twelve men he'd sent for on it.

He hoped Clint Adams had gotten nice and comfortable out in the sheepherders' camp.

TWENTY-FOUR

Henry John alerted Clint by clapping his hands together. Clint looked away from the sheep and saw a rider approaching. He watched until the rider was close enough to identify.

"That's Dr. Travis," Terry said.

"I know."

"I wonder what she wants."

"I guess we'll have to wait until she tells us," Clint said.

He was surprised to see Randi riding toward them, but the surprise was a pleasant one—at least, he hoped it would be.

"Good afternoon," she called to them.

"Hello, Doctor," Terry said.

Clint didn't know whether it was conscious or unconscious, but Terry moved her horse closer to his. He was sure that Randi had noticed it.

"What can we do for you?"

"Actually, Miss Haslett," Randi said, "I rode out here to talk to Clint."

"So, talk," Terry said.

Randi looked at Clint and said, "Is there somewhere we can talk . . . alone?"

"Sure," Clint said. "I'll ride around to the other side of the flock, Terry."

That was the first time he had said *flock* on the first try, instead of *herd*.

"Suit yourself," Terry said. She and Randi matched stares until Randi turned her horse to ride alongside Clint.

"I see things have progressed," Randi said to him.

"What do you mean?"

"Don't tell me you don't know that woman is in love with you?"

"That's silly."

"No," Randi said. "What's silly is you pretending it isn't so."

"She's become attached to me because I'm helping her," he said.

"Helping her how?" she asked. "From what I hear around town, Tom Lord and his men haven't been anywhere near you all week."

"You sound disappointed," he said. "You're the one who warned me that this was dangerous."

"It is . . . but it has been quiet, hasn't it?"

"The calm before the storm," he said. "Lord will send Pace and his new men out here soon enough."

"New men?"

"Have you seen any new men in town?"

"No, none . . . but I did see Sam Pace riding in as I was on my way out here."

"Is there a stage due today?"

"I believe there is."

"He may be meeting it."

"Because there are new men on it?"

He nodded.

"How do you know?"

He explained what he thought was Tom Lord's strategy in leaving them alone for a week.

"Maybe he's just decided to give up?"

"You know Tom Lord better than I do, Randi," Clint said. "What do you think?"

"Not likely."

"So what really brought you out here?" he asked.

Without hesitation—which surprised her as much as it did him—she said, "I've been thinking about you."

"And I've been thinking about you."

"Really?" she said. "Have you had the time?"

"Randi—"

"This was foolish."

"Why?"

"Because I'm not good at this," she said. "And I didn't think that seeing you with Terry Haslett would . . . bother me."

"I'm glad it does."

"You are an infuriating man."

They had been drifting around the flock, and now Clint called Duke to a halt. He turned in his saddle to face her.

"Randi," he said, "when this is over I'd like to come

back to town, stay a while, and have us get to know each other."

"I don't know if I can wait that long, Clint," she said. "Besides, looking at the situation realistically, when this thing is over you may not be alive."

"Some people would call that looking at things pessimistically."

"Call it whatever you want," she said. "Are you sleeping with her?"

Clint was glad she had asked the question that way, and not have you *ever* slept with her. "No," he answered.

"I guess I'll have to believe you."

"Only if you want to."

"I do."

Clint leaned over, and Randi did the same, so they could kiss. He wondered if Terry could see them, and hoped she couldn't.

"What prompted you to come out here?" he asked.

"A friend of mine gave me some advice," she said. "Can you come to town later?"

"Sure," he said. With a week gone by he figured it was time he put in an appearance in town. He was sure that Lord knew he was still around, but riding into town would make it a certainty. Besides, he was interested in who got off that stage today.

"You go on back and I'll be along a little later."

"All right," she said. She reached out her hand and he took it and held it briefly.

"I'm sorry for the things I said—"

"Forget it," he said. "I'll see you in town."

She nodded and rode off. He watched her for a few

moments, then wheeled Duke around and rode back to Terry.

"You seem pretty friendly with the doctor," Terry said. She didn't look happy.

"I'm a friendly guy, Terry," he said. "I'll be riding into town later on."

"To be with her?"

"There's a stage coming in today," he said. "I want to see who's on it."

"Sure," she said. "You go ahead, we can do without you."

"I'll be back this evening."

"Uh-huh," she said, turning her horse. "Suit yourself, do what you want. I don't care."

He stared after her in puzzlement. For a woman who *didn't* want to be with him, she was getting pretty worked up over a woman who did.

TWENTY-FIVE

It took Joe Lang a long time to make up his mind, but he finally rode into town from the Lord ranch to see Tom Lord. He didn't want Mrs. Lord to see him talking to her husband.

Lang presented himself to Kelly Harlowe and announced that he wanted to see Lord.

Kelly liked old Joe Lang. He was the only man she knew who didn't look at her like she was a sandwich and he was a starving man.

Well, except for Clint Adams, but she knew Adams liked the way she looked. Joe Lang never gave her that impression. . . .

"I'll tell him, Joe," she said.

"Thanks, Miss Harlowe."

She went into Lord's office and said, "Joe is here to see you."

133

She was surprised to see a look of affection cross Lord's face.

"Send him right in, Kelly."

Clint rode into town warily. He hadn't been there for the better part of a week, and a quiet week it had been. He didn't know what Lord and his men might have planned for him.

As he rode past the stage stop he exchanged long glances with Sam Pace, and if he needed proof that some hired talent was coming in on the stage, Pace's presence was it. The man was obviously waiting for the stage.

Clint rode to the livery and turned Duke over to the liveryman.

"Thought you'd left us fer good," the man said.

"Not yet," Clint said. "But hopefully soon."

As Clint walked away the liveryman said to Duke, "I hope it ain't feet first."

Lord listened to what old Joe Lang had to say to him, and then put his hand on the man's shoulder.

"Thanks for telling me this, Joe."

"I hated like hell t'do it, Tom, but we been friends a long time . . ."

"Yes, we have, Joe," Lord said. "Thank you. Go on back to the ranch now."

"What are you gonna do about it, Tom?"

"I'm going to take care of it, Joe," Tom Lord said. "I'm going to take care of it."

After Joe Lang left Kelly heard Tom Lord laughing in his office. The laughter was so uncontrolled that she had to go in and see what was going on.

Lord was seated at his desk, both hands holding his belly, as he continued to laugh.

"What was that all about?" she asked.

Lord was still laughing too hard to answer.

"Thomas Lord," she said, "stop laughing and answer me. What did that old man have to say that was so funny?"

"He . . . he . . . he," Lord stammered, trying to regain control of himself, "he wanted to tell me that my . . . my wife and my . . . my foreman are sleeping together . . ."

Kelly stared at Lord for a moment, and then started laughing herself. . . .

Clint walked to Dr. Randi Travis's office and knocked on the door. She was smiling when she opened the door, and he slipped in past her.

"Are you hiding from someone?" she asked, closing the door behind him.

He went to her window and looked out, but he couldn't see the stage stop from there.

"Have you got a window I can see the stage stop from?" he asked.

"Sure I do," she said, eyeing him. "It's upstairs . . . in my bedroom."

After Lord and Kelly had gotten their laughter under control she poured them both a brandy.

"The poor cow," he said. "She thinks she's sneaking around behind my back and even old half-blind Joe Lang knows what's going on. My God," he said, in danger of giving into waves of uncontrollable laughter again, "the whole ranch must know!"

"What can Pace see in her?" Kelly asked.

"What can he see?" Lord asked. "My dear Kelly, you surprise me. He sees the same thing in her that you see in me."

She frowned and said, "What's that?"

"My money, dear."

"Now Tom—"

"Never mind denying it, my dear," he said, waving a hand at her. "I accept it as a fact. I certainly don't mind paying you to let me into your bed. You're worth every penny of it."

"I'm not a common whore, Tom," she said haughtily.

"No, Kelly," he said, raising his glass to her, "if there's anything you aren't, it's common. Now, finish your brandy and let's get back to work."

She drank her brandy and as she went back to her desk she heard him begin to laugh again.

Sam Pace saw Clint Adams go down the alley toward Dr. Travis's office. Pace was convinced that Adams was sleeping with both bitches—the sheepherder and the doctor—while he had to settle for Tom Lord's cast-off wife.

That would change, he thought. When he had the money, and the ranch, that would change.

Clint undressed Randi Travis as if she were a birthday present. He peeled her clothing from her slowly, exposing her flesh little by little. When her breasts were bare he eyed them appreciatively. For a woman in her forties—or any age, for that matter—she had fine, rounded, firm breasts. He palmed them, feeling the nipples harden, and then leaned forward to lick them. She leaned into him, groaning, running her fingers through his hair.

Still kissing her breasts he removed the rest of her clothes and pushed her back on her bed.

"Hurry," she said to him. Galvanized into action, he stood up, removed his clothes, and joined her on the bed.

They kissed and explored each other with their hands, and then she turned him over so that she could straddle him. She didn't take him inside yet, just pinned his hard penis between them, rubbing his chest with her hands. She leaned over, tongued his nipples, and then traced a wet path down his belly until she had him in her mouth.

She rode him wetly with her mouth, moaning, cupping his balls gently, running her nails along the length of him as he slid from her mouth.

He thought she was going to finish him that way, but abruptly she released him, straddled him, and this time took him inside. She was slick and hot and as she came down on him he groaned. She looked down at him, spreading both her hands on his chest, and then began to ride up and down on him. He reached for her breasts, squeezed, and fondled them as she quickened her pace, taking them both to the point where neither would have control over the situation. . . .

TWENTY-SIX

Naked and huddled inside a blanket, Clint and Randi watched the stage stop from her window.

"You're going to have to get back, aren't you?" she asked. "I mean, Terry will be expecting you, won't she?"

"I'm sure she will," he said, "and yes, I will have to get back, but I'm real interested to see who gets off that stage."

"Why?"

He looked at her and said, "Being a gun for hire puts you in a pretty small club, Randi. Most of them know each other, and because of the kind of life I've led, I know a lot of them."

"You mean you might know some of the men who are coming here to work for Tom Lord?"

"I might."

"Well, that would be good, wouldn't it?" she asked.

"I mean, if they're friends of yours they won't—"

"I said I might know them," Clint said, cutting her off. "I didn't say they would be friends of mine."

"Oh," she said, blinking rapidly. "Of course, how silly of me. You'd know who they are, but they wouldn't necessarily have friendly intentions toward you."

"It really doesn't matter, you know," he said. "Some of these men would kill a friend for the right price. In fact, some of them would kill their own mothers."

He felt her shudder against him, and slipped an arm around her. As he did so they saw the stage coming down the main street.

"Here we go," he said, and they both turned their attention to the stage.

As they watched, five passengers got off. One was a woman, who Sam Pace assisted in stepping down from the stage. One was an older man carrying as drummer's case.

The other three spoke to Pace, who nodded and shook their hands enthusiastically.

"There we go," Clint said. "Three."

"That's not so many . . . is it?" Randi asked.

"It might just be the first batch," Clint said, "and some of them will ride in on their own."

Clint got a good look at all of them while they waited for their belongings to be tossed down from atop the stage.

"Do you know any of them?" she asked.

"No," Clint said, with certainty. "I don't know any of the three."

As he watched, the three men followed Sam Pace,

and it was clear that their destination was the hotel owned by Tom Lord.

He stood up, leaving the blanket to Randi while he padded naked across the floor to her bed and collected his clothes. She watched, holding the blanket tightly around her while he dressed.

"Where are you going?"

"Back to the sheep camp," he said. "I doubt that Pace will put these men into immediate action. He'll probably want to wait until more of them arrive, but then you never know."

When he was dressed she stood up, still holding the blanket around her.

"I'm glad . . ." she said, haltingly, unsure of how to put her feelings into words, " . . . that we had this . . . chance to . . . to . . ."

"Get to know each other better?"

"Yes."

He smiled at her and said, "So am I, Randi. Um, would you mind if I came by again, after this was all over?"

"No," she said, "I wouldn't mind at all."

As he went out the door she said to herself, "As long as you're still around when this is all over."

Suddenly, she got an idea, and began to dress.

Clint walked quickly toward the hotel and watched from across the street. He could see through the front door that Sam Pace was registering the three men, and giving them their room keys. Before they did anything, the men would want to rest, freshen up, and have a meal. They would also want to get the lay of the land before they made any kind of move. Clint certainly had time to ride back out to the sheepherders' camp—but his curiosity was getting the better of him. He didn't recognize any of the three men, but he might recognize their names. If he knew who they were, he would be better prepared to face them.

He started across the street.

Further down the street Randi Travis was standing across the street from Tom Lord's office. It had been years since she had been inside the building. She could still remember vividly the last time she had been there. After that encounter with Tom Lord in his office she had sworn never to go there again, but she felt that now she had a good enough reason to enter it again.

She started across. . . .

TWENTY-SEVEN

When Kelly Harlowe looked up from her desk and saw Dr. Randi Travis standing in the doorway, she tried to hide the surprise she felt.

"Doctor," she said.

"Hello, Kelly."

To Kelly it looked as if Dr. Travis was very uncomfortable about being there.

"Can I help you?" she asked Randi.

"Is he in?"

"Mr. Lord?"

"Yes."

"You want to see him?" She wasn't quite able to hide the surprise from her voice.

Randi hesitated before answering, "Yes."

Kelly stared at her for a few moments, then stood up and said, "I'll tell him."

• • •

Clint walked up to the front desk and the clerk said, "Can I help you?"

"Yes," Clint said. "The three men who just entered, I thought I knew one of them. Would you know their names?"

"Well, of course I would," the clerk said. "They registered, didn't they?"

"May I see their names?" Clint asked.

When the clerk hesitated Clint took out a dollar and handed it to the man. The dollar quickly disappeared, and the register was turned his way. He read the three newly written-in names: Lou Palmer, Dale Decatur, and Dean Teacher.

Teacher was the only name he recognized.

"Thanks," Clint said, and left the hotel before Pace or any of his guests could come down.

Dean Teacher had a reputation as a fast and accurate man with a gun—a gun that was always for hire.

When Kelly came back out of Lord's office she said, "Mr. Lord will see you, Doctor."

"Thank you."

"Go ahead in."

Again, Randi hesitated, then took a deep breath and entered Tom Lord's office.

When Randi entered his office Tom Lord could scarcely believe his eyes. The last time was still vivid in his mind, and she had sworn that she would never enter it again. Not that he could blame her. It was the only time in his life he had lost his head and tried to force himself on a woman.

Or, to be more precise, the only time he had ever tried to rape a woman.

Clint walked to the livery to saddle Duke and head back to the camp. If Dean Teacher was here, the chances were very good that he would be the head of the group that Pace and Lord would send against him. Pace was just a foreman, so he would not be chosen to lead, and it was unlikely that they would hire a second man of Dean Teacher's abilities and reputation. There would be too much conflict there.

Already, Clint was starting to think that maybe there was a way to nip Lord's plan in the bud.

"What brings you here, Randi . . . after all this time?" Lord asked.

Randi started to speak, then turned and closed the office door. The move started her heart pounding wildly. She remembered the last time she was in the office with Lord, with the door closed.

Abruptly, she took a deep breath and turned to face him.

Dean Teacher looked out the window of his room at the town of Lords. Clint Adams was here somewhere, and Teacher itched to face him. Over the years Adams had met and vanquished many a man with a reputation, and for years Teacher had been following the exploits of the Gunsmith. Over the last few years, however, Adams had managed to keep a different sort of profile. No longer was his reputation for his gun so much as it was for his intervention into the lives of people in need. That was why Teacher knew, when Pace contacted him, that this was just that sort of situation. Adams was definitely here, and here was where he was going to finally meet his match in a man called Dean Teacher.

"I want you to leave Terry Haslett alone," Randi said.

"Really?" Lord said. "That's why you're here?"

"Yes."

"To intervene on behalf of a sheepherder?" Lord asked. "I don't think so."

"Thomas—"

"You're here because of Adams," Lord said, "not because of Terry Haslett and her sheep."

Randi decided not to waste time denying it.

"You're bringing killers into Lords," she said. "Are you prepared to deal with them after they've done their job?"

"You mean after they've killed Adams?"

"These men are reprehensible," Randi said. "What makes you think they're just going to leave after it's all over?"

"What do you mean?"

"I mean," Randi said, "you've built this town up into something you can be proud of. What if these men decide to . . . to loot it? What will you do then?"

He smiled at her, a condescending smile that infuriated her.

"These men work for me," he said. "Nothing like that will happen."

Randi placed both of her hands on his desk and glared at him.

"I don't want anything to happen to Clint Adams."

"Really?" he asked. He also leaned over, bringing his face close to hers. "And what are you willing to give to make sure that nothing does happen to him?"

She stood up and backed away from him.

"I could still bring charges against you . . . for what happened last time."

He laughed then, and she suddenly knew that she had made a terrible mistake in coming here.

"You would have to explain to a judge why you waited over three years to bring those charges," he said. "And besides, who would you tell? The sheriff?"

"He's in your pocket," she said, "just as the judge would be."

"Randi—" Lord began, coming around his desk.

Randi suddenly felt panicky and penned in.

"Don't," she said, backing away from him. "Don't come any closer."

"You know I want you . . ."

"You have Kelly, now," Randi said, her back coming in contact with the door.

"But you're the one I really want, Randi," he said, still advancing on her. "I've never made a secret of that. Everyone knows that . . . even my wife."

"Thomas, no—"

"You came here, Randi," he said. "Remember?"

She turned then and quickly opened the door and ran out through it, past Kelly's desk. Kelly watched her run through the outer door, then turned and saw Lord step out of his office, staring after the doctor.

After a moment, Lord looked at Kelly, catching her looking at him.

"Have any of the men arrived yet?"

"You'd have to ask Pace."

"Get him," Lord said, and went back to his office.

Kelly decided that she was going to have to ask Lord to station a man in the office, just so she could send him to find Pace every time Lord wanted him.

TWENTY-EIGHT

As Clint rode back into camp he was pleased to see that things had not changed much since he had left. Margarite was sitting at the fire, tending to dinner. He assumed that Henry John and Terry were out with the sheep.

He dismounted, saw to Duke's needs, and then walked up to the fire. The young girl wasted no time in handing him a cup of coffee.

"You're enough to spoil a man, Margarite," he said, accepting it.

She looked away shyly, and did not answer.

Clint sat there, drinking the coffee, until Terry rode into camp.

"Where's Henry John?" he asked.

"Still with the sheep."

He finished his coffee and stood up.

"I'll go out and help him."

"Did you see your doctor friend?" Terry asked.

He turned to face her and said, "Yes, I did."

"Anything else of interest happen?" Terry asked. She had a pair of black leather gloves on, and she pulled them off and accepted a cup of coffee from Margarite.

"As a matter if fact, it did," Clint said. "Three men arrived in town. They were met at the stage by Sam Pace."

"Three gunmen?"

Clint nodded.

"Do you know who they are?"

"I didn't recognize any of them," Clint said, "but I checked them out. I knew only one man. His name is Dean Teacher."

"Teacher?" she asked. "Do I know that name?"

"You've probably heard it," Clint said. "He's for hire, and he's good."

"How good?"

"Extremely good."

"Better than you?"

"Now, there's only one way to tell that, isn't there?" he asked.

"I don't know, Clint," she said. "I don't know about these things. What are you going to do now?"

"I don't know," he said. "The others should be arriving soon. We should probably make a move before that happens. Once they're here in full force, with Teacher to lead them, they be difficult to deal with."

"Difficult to deal with?" she repeated. "Is that all

you can say about a dozen men who might be here just to kill you?"

"All right," he said. "*Very* difficult to deal with. What's put a burr under your saddle?"

"Nothing," she said, biting the word off. "Nothing at all. Maybe I just don't like the idea of you being killed over a few sheep."

"You don't seem to mind being killed over a few sheep," he pointed out.

"But they're my sheep," she said.

"I guess that would make a difference," he said. "Look, Terry, don't worry, I don't intend to die over a few sheep."

"You're going to kill twelve men?"

"I may not have to."

"You have a plan?"

"I have something in mind," he said, "but I have to think about it a while. Let me go out and relieve Henry John a while, and maybe I'll be able to explain it all better later."

"All right."

"I'll have some of that hot stew later, Margarite," he said.

"I'll save it," she assured him.

Clint left the camp, mounted Duke and rode out to the sheep.

"You like him."

Margarite looked across the fire at Terry while the older woman considered the question.

"I suppose," Terry finally said, grudgingly.

"I like him," Margarite said.

"I know."

Terry stared at Margarite then and saw the look on the young girl's face.

"Oh," she said, "you mean, you *like* him."

Margarite nodded, and then shyly looked away.

"Well, forget about it, Margarite," Terry said, maybe too harshly. "He's got himself a woman in town."

"The doctor?"

"Yes."

Margarite thought a moment, then said, "She's a nice woman. I like her."

Terry hesitated a moment, then said, "Yes, dammit, so do I."

Later, while Margarite was sleeping, Terry once again asked herself the same question. Yes, she did like Clint Adams, she liked him more than she wanted to admit. She liked him so much that she hated the thought of him being in bed with Randi Travis, even though she liked Dr. Travis.

Still, she had been to bed with him before Randi, hadn't she? And she had proceeded to let him know that she didn't want to do it again—when she actually did.

If Clint Adams preferred the older woman to her, then Terry Haslett only had herself to blame.

Still again, where was Clint now? Was he in town with Randi Travis? No, he was out here with her. In fact, he had probably left Randi's bed to come out here to her, so who did that mean Clint Adams preferred?

Maybe, she told herself, maybe she ought to just ask him.

Clint could make out Henry John's silhouette on the other side of the flock. The mute boy waved, and Clint waved back. Clint wished that Henry John could hear and talk. He wished he had someone he could talk to, someone to bounce ideas off of so he could listen to them coming back at him.

As it stood now, he could only think of one way to stop Tom Lord before he got his gang of gunmen rolling. It was the same way you killed a snake—by cutting off the head.

TWENTY-NINE

Tom Lord stared across his desk at Sam Pace.

"How many men have arrived?"

"Three on the stage," Pace said, "including Dean Teacher."

"He's the one you were raving about."

"If anyone can get rid of Adams, it's Teacher," Pace said. "He's got a rep that's been growing and growing."

"Who else is here?"

"A couple of useful gun hands named Lou Palmer and Dale Decatur."

"Useful?"

"They'll be good backups for Teacher, and they'll follow him."

"Will the others, when they arrive?"

"Teacher commands that kind of respect," Pace assured his boss. "The other men we're waiting for are varied in talent, but none can match Teacher. They'll all follow him, boss. I'm sure of it."

"When will they be getting in?"

"Probably over the next two days."

"That's good," Lord said. "We've left Terry Haslett and her sheep alone long enough. It's time for us to make our position abundantly clear."

"We'll do that, for sure," Pace said.

"I don't want the women killed, is that understood?"

"Yes sir. What about the mute?"

"I don't care what happens to him."

"And Adams?"

"Let Dean Teacher do to him whatever comes natural."

Pace smiled and said, "Yes sir."

Early the next morning two men rode into town side by side. They were Aaron Kincaid and his sidekick, Frank Bernard. They fell into the same category as Lou Palmer and Dale Decatur—useful men with a gun.

Just after the noon hour, a lone man in black rode in. He was dressed like a gambler, and liked people to call him Lucky. His real name was Stanley Weeks—which explained why he liked to be call Lucky. He was a fair hand with a gun, but what he lacked in marksmanship he made up for in pure meanness.

Just before three o'clock three men rode in together. Two of them had traveled over fifty miles together. They were Tully Blanchard and Dutch Mantel. They wore guns, but both were big men and they were known to do more damage with their fists.

They had met Bill Ransom just outside of town. Ransom's weapon was a knife, and he made sure he was never without one. In a specially built rig he carried six throwing knives crisscrossing his chest, and a huge bowie knife on his belt.

"How many men are here now?" Lord asked Pace.

It was a full twenty hours since they'd had this kind of conversation. At that time only Teacher, Palmer, and Decatur were present. Now there was triple that.

"We have nine men," Pace said.

"Are they all prepared to follow Teacher?"

"I talked to all of them, and they all agree that Teacher is the man to lead them."

"How many more are we expecting?"

"Maybe three or four, if they show up. Today was the day they were all supposed to show up, but there might be more tomorrow."

Lord thought the situation over. Nine men against Adams, a mute boy, and two women seemed to be pretty good odds, but where was the harm in waiting one more day, just to see who else would arrive.

"All right," Lord said. "We'll wait one more day."

"Whatever you say, boss."

"Just make sure these men stay out of trouble," Lord warned his foreman. "They're your responsibility."

"I thought they'd be Teacher's responsibility."

Lord stared hard at Pace and said, "Let's put it this way, Sam. The other men are Teacher's responsibility, but Teacher had better know that he reports to you, and you report to me. Understand? *He's* your responsibility."

"I understand."

"If anything goes wrong," Lord said, "I'm going to hold you responsible."

Pace shrugged and said, "What could go wrong?"

"So what could go wrong?" Kelly Harlowe asked later that night in her hotel room.

"We're dealing with Clint Adams, the Gunsmith," Tom Lord reminded her. He was stroking her bare back because he loved the smoothness of her skin. Compared to Kelly, his wife had skin like a lizard. "With a man like that, anything can happen."

"But you've got ten men to send against him," Kelly said. She was counting Sam Pace among them.

"Maybe more, come tomorrow."

"And you're leaving Sam Pace in charge?" she asked. "When you know that he's sleeping with your wife behind your back?"

"He *thinks* he's been sleeping with my wife behind my back," Lord corrected her, laughing shortly. "Actually, I'm glad he's been keeping the bitch off my back—but don't you worry about Sam Pace, Kelly." Lord reached around in front and cupped Kelly's full breasts in both hands, pressing her large nipples with his thumbs.

Kelly closed her eyes for a moment, knowing that

she was going to have to perform. Lord's touch was about as gentle as a bear's.

"I have something special planned for my loyal foreman," Lord said, squeezing her.

She put a smile on her face and said, "Not like the something special you've got planned for me, I hope?" turning into him.

THIRTY

"I'll be going into town tomorrow morning," Clint told Terry.

They had just finished their dinner and were drinking coffee. Henry John and his sister were out with the sheep.

"Will you be coming back?" she asked.

"That might not be up to me."

"Who, then?"

"Lord, and his men."

"Are you going after them?"

"I'm going to go and see Dean Teacher."

"You mean you're going to kill him."

"Not if I don't have to."

"And if he kills you?"

"Then I'd suggest you move your sheep, Terry," Clint said.

"I'm tired of moving my sheep, Clint," she said. "Every time I move them I lose some."

"If you stay here," he said, "you might just lose all of them."

"I'm going with you tomorrow."

"Oh no, you're not."

"Yes, I am," she said. "I'm the reason you're going against these killers. I want to be there."

"It's too dangerous."

She leaned forward and said, "I'll bring a rifle."

"Terry—"

"If you don't take me with you," she said, "I'll follow you, anyway."

He stared at her for a few moments, and then shrugged. He knew she meant it.

"All right," he said. "Turn in, we'll get an early start."

She nodded, and went into her tent.

Clint stayed up longer, thinking about tomorrow. He didn't know how many men Lord had lined up, but he figured he'd be riding into at least a dozen guns. A man like Dean Teacher, though, he'd have to make at least one try by himself, just to add to his reputation.

Clint was counting on that.

Sam Pace sat on the edge of Olivia Lord's bed. Behind him she was pressing her sagging breasts against his back in an attempt to excite him.

"What's wrong, Sam?" she asked.

"I'm just thinking about tomorrow."

"What about tomorrow."

He looked at her over his shoulder.

"Tomorrow's the day your husband meets with an accident."

Excitedly she said, "Tomorrow?"

"That's right."

"Who's going to do it?"

"One of the men we hired."

"Which one?"

"That's not important, Olivia," Pace said.

"Are you sure you can trust him?"

"Oh, I can trust him," Pace said. "I gave him half the money you gave me, and promised him the other half when the job was done."

She slid off the bed and got on her knees in front of him.

"Tomorrow, we'll be free, Sam," she said. "It will be just you and me . . . and Tom's money."

"Yeah, right," Pace said, "and the money."

She lowered her head and he felt her hot mouth on him. He closed his eyes and pretended it was Kelly Harlowe taking him into her mouth, *her* hand cupping his balls, *her* moans as she sucked on him, *her* red hair he was tangling his hands in, and *her* mouth he was exploding into. . . .

THIRTY-ONE

Tom Lord was looking out his window when Clint Adams and Terry Haslett rode into town.

"Well, I'll be damned."

"What is it?" Kelly asked. She had been putting some papers on Lord's desk.

"Look at this," Lord said.

She moved next to him and looked out the window.

"We don't have to go looking for him," Lord said. "Adams is coming to us."

"Yeah," Kelly said, looking at Lord, "but why?"

Lord looked at her and then said, "That's a good question. Is Pace in town yet?"

"He rode in early this morning."

"All right," Lord said, "get him."

"Hey, Teacher."

There weren't enough rooms in the hotel to go around, so Teacher and the others had to double up.

Teacher was sharing a room with the knife man, Bill Ransom. Ransom was standing at the window.

"What is it?"

"Come and take a look."

Teacher stood up and walked to the window.

"Am I mistaken," Ransom asked, "or is that Clint Adams?"

Teacher looked down at the street and saw a man and a woman riding by.

"That's him, all right."

"And that must be the sheep lady," Ransom said. "Not bad, huh?"

"How do you know Adams on sight?" Teacher asked Bill Ransom.

"Huh? Oh, I seen him before, once or twice."

"He ever see you?"

Ransom laughed.

"He don't me from a hole in the ground."

"Good," Teacher said. "Go and make sure everyone is awake. I want to talk to them."

"Sure, Teacher."

"Tell them I want to see them in the restaurant downstairs."

Ransom nodded, and left the room.

"The Gunsmith is in town," Teacher announced to the nine men he had been put in charge of. He and the men were the only ones in the hotel dining room.

"Good," Tully Blanchard said. "That'll save us the trouble of going looking for him."

"Are we gonna take him while he's in town?" Dutch Mantel asked.

"That's why I asked you all to come down here," Teacher said. "To tell you exactly what we're going to do . . ."

"Adams is in town," Lord said to Pace. "I want him taken care of while he's here."

"Where is he, exactly?" Pace asked.

"I don't know," Lord said. "He might have taken his horse to the livery. Find him."

"All right."

"He's got Terry Haslett with him," Lord said as Pace headed for the door. "I don't want her hurt . . . not yet, anyway."

"I know," Pace said, "I know. I'll take care of it."

"Yeah," Tom Lord said. "You do that, Sam."

Yeah, Sam Pace thought on his way downstairs. Everything was going to be taken care of today.

Everything.

When Pace entered the hotel he saw Teacher and the other men in the dining room.

"What's going on?"

"Adams is in town," Teacher said.

"I know," Pace said. "I was coming to tell you. Mr. Lord wants him taken care of, today."

"That's what I intend to do," Teacher said. "We were just going over our . . . plan."

"And what is the plan?"

"I'm going to take Adams," Teacher said.

"Alone?"

"Alone."

"What about the rest of these guys?"

"If Adams kills me, these guys can have their turn at him."

"That's crazy," Pace said. "Why face him alone when you've got all this help."

"Because," Teacher said, giving Pace a hard look, "I can take him."

"Oh, Jesus—" Pace started. "Do you know how many dead men have said the same thing?"

"Pace," Teacher said, "I'm going after Adams alone, and I'll kill the first man who lifts a hand against him before I do. Do you understand that?"

"Sure," Pace said. "Sure, Teacher, I understand. You want to get yourself killed, you go right ahead."

Teacher poked Pace in the chest and said, "I'll be back to see you, after."

As Teacher left the hotel Pace turned to face the other men.

"Are you men ready to earn your money?"

They all nodded.

"I got a question," Bill Ransom said.

"What's the question?" Pace asked.

"If Teacher kills Adams himself," Ransom asked, "do we all still get paid?"

It was a good question, and standing there in front of the nine men, Pace could only think of one answer.

"As long as Clint Adams is dead by the end of the day," he said, "everyone gets paid."

"Well, I don't know about the rest of you," Ransom said, standing up, "but I don't want to miss *this*."

They all stood up and followed Ransom out into the hotel lobby. Pace grabbed the arm of one of the men as he passed.

"Are you ready to earn your money?" he asked.

"Don't worry," the man said, grinning wolfishly. "I'm ready."

THIRTY-TWO

Clint and Terry left their horses at the livery. As they were leaving she grabbed his arm.

"What are you going to do now?"

"Now all I have to do is walk down the street," Clint said. "Teacher will find me."

"What makes you so sure he'll try to kill you alone, without the others?"

"I don't know who all of the others are," Clint said, "but I doubt that any of them will have the reputation that Dean Teacher does. A man with a reputation like that will do anything he can to enhance it."

"What about you?" she asked. "Do you want to enhance your reputation?"

"My reputation is something I haven't entirely earned, Terry."

"What makes you think the same isn't true of Dean Teacher?"

He stared at her and realized that she was right. He was judging the man solely from his reputation, and he hated when people did that to him.

Well, it was too late to do anything about it now.

"I'm going to walk down the center of the street," Clint told Terry. "Stay to one side, Terry, and for God's sake, stay out of the way."

"Sure," she said. "I'll stay out of the way."

Randi Travis was on her way to the general store when she saw a group of men come out of the hotel owned by Tom Lord. They were all wearing guns, except for one man, who was wearing a lot of knives.

Something was happening, and she had a feeling that it was going to involve Clint Adams.

That was when she saw Clint walk up the street from the direction of the livery stable.

She ran across the street to the sheriff's office. Sheriff Haywood looked up in surprise as she burst into the room.

"Sheriff, you've got to do something," she said. "They're going to kill him."

"Now hold on, Doctor," Haywood said. "Who is going to kill who?"

"Tom Lord's men are going to kill Clint Adams."

"What? When? Where?"

"Now, out there on the street!" she said, pointing behind her.

"Well, damn," he said, standing up.

"What are you going to do about it?"

"Well, I sure as hell ain't gonna miss it, that's for sure."

The sheriff moved to his window and looked outside.

"You mean you're just going to stay in here and watch?" she demanded.

"That's exactly what I'm gonna do, Doctor," he said. "Was I you, I'd find myself a window and watch from inside, too. There's gonna be plenty of lead flyin' out there real soon."

"You're a disgrace!" she said, and turned and ran out.

"Yes, ma'am," he said to her back. "But I'm a live disgrace, and I'm gonna stay that way."

Tom Lord watched from his window as eight men exited his hotel. He had seen Teacher come out alone, and watched now to see how the other men were going to be deployed. He was surprised to see that they simply spread out on the boardwalk in front of the hotel. He would have thought that a man of Teacher's reputation would think of a more imaginative way to set them up.

"Is it happening?" Kelly asked from behind him.

"Any minute," he said. "Come watch."

One part of her didn't want to watch, but the other part was too fascinated not to.

"Where's Adams?" she asked.

Lord hesitated a moment, then said, "There, coming up the street."

"Jesus," she said. "He's walking right down the center of the street. Does he think he can beat them all?"

"Maybe," Lord said, "he just wants to go out in a blaze of glory."

"Where's the other man?" Kelly asked. "Where's Teacher?"

Lord looked around, then frowned and said, "I don't know . . . wait! There he is. What the hell does he think he's doing?"

Dean Teacher was standing directly below Tom Lord's window, which was why Lord couldn't see him. When he spotted Clint Adams walking up the street, he stepped off the boardwalk and moved to the center of the street to wait.

Clint saw Dean Teacher standing in the center of the street and heaved a sigh of relief. In this case, at least, the man was living up to the reputation.

Terry Haslett and her rifle were on the opposite side of the street from the eight hired killers. When she saw Dean Teacher walk out into the center of the street, she stopped walking and sought some cover. If anything happened to Clint, all she knew was that she was going to start shooting.

Meanwhile Randi Travis ran back to her office and retrieved her Winchester from a corner of the room. She hadn't fired it in a very long time, but she remembered how. She only hoped it wouldn't explode in her hands.

The man Sam Pace had hired to kill Tom Lord looked up and saw Lord standing in his window. He made a perfect target, and when the shooting started, the man was going to earn his money.

THIRTY-THREE

Teacher was relaxed. He was always relaxed before he faced a man down. Dean Teacher had resigned himself long ago to the fact that when he died he would do so facedown in some dusty street, with a better man standing in front of him. For that reason he was never nervous in situations like this. He expected a better man to kill him, he just hoped that it wouldn't happen for a long, long time.

Clint could see how relaxed Teacher was. He knew then that Teacher would be good. Here was a man who—like himself—was resigned to the fact that he would die by a bullet.

A man who wasn't afraid to die was a very dangerous man.

All of the onlookers held their breaths as the distance between the two men lessened. It was only

Clint Adams who was moving. Dean Teacher was just standing there, waiting for him.

They didn't speak.

There was nothing to say. They both knew why they were there.

Clint stood easily, his feet spread slightly, watching Teacher closely. Sometimes, you could tell by watching a man's eyes when he was going to make his move. Sometimes, you watched his shoulders.

This time, Clint knew he was going to have to rely on pure instinct.

Sheep, he thought. Damned stupid things for people to be dying over.

Teacher watched Clint Adams closely. The man standing in front of him had a reputation second to none. If Teacher could kill him, then someone would soon be thinking the same thing about him.

He went for his gun.

As Teacher drew his gun, Clint eased his from his holster. At the sound of the shots he did not even look to see who was still standing. He simply raised his gun and fired. . . .

At the sound of the shots Terry Haslett raised her rifle and aimed it at the men across the street. When one of them fired, she started to squeeze the trigger. . . .

From further down the street, on the same side as Terry, Randi Travis raised her rifle and pointed it at the group of men in front of the hotel. . . .

The glass in Tom Lord's window shattered and the hand-painted lettering that said Tom Lord, Ltd. fell in shards to the street below. Some of then fell into the office, and Kelly Harlowe felt them stinging her face. She turned to say something to Tom Lord, but he wasn't there anymore. He had toppled forward and followed most of the glass down to the street below.

Kelly Harlowe screamed. . . .

Clint fired and saw the bullet strike Teacher in the chest. Teacher's bullet whizzed by his ear, coming very close. As Teacher started to fall he heard the other shooting. He looked up in time to see Tom Lord fall from his window.

When Tom Lord hit the ground, it caught everyone's attention, as did Kelly Harlowe's ear-shattering scream. . . .

Clint quickly sized up the situation and knew he had to act fast to prevent a massacre.

"Don't anyone fire!" he shouted. "Hold your fire, all of you!"

Everyone's eyes moved from the body of Tom Lord to the standing figure of Clint Adams. It was then they realized that Dean Teacher was no longer standing.

The other men looked at each other, as if asking, what's next?

Clint walked over to Tom Lord, leaned over him and determined that he was dead. He stood up and faced the hired men.

"Tom Lord is dead," he called out. "There's no payday here, anymore. How many of you want to die for nothing?"

"Not me," Bill Ransom said, and then the men around him nodded.

Sam Pace came out of the hotel and saw Clint Adams still standing. He also saw that Adams had taken charge of the situation.

If I kill Adams, he thought, everyone will start shooting. To him, it was a perfect way to get rid of some of the hired men without paying them.

After all, it was his money, now.

He drew his gun and pointed it at Clint Adams.

Both Terry and Randi saw Sam Pace point his gun at Clint, and they fired at the same time. One bullet struck the front of the hotel. The other hit Pace, knocking him through the hotel window.

Nobody else fired.

THIRTY-FOUR

Before leaving Lords, Clint had a lot of people to see. . . .

The day after the shooting Clint rode out to the sheepherders' camp.

"You're leaving?" Terry asked.

"Yes."

"I feel . . . very foolish . . ."

"About what?"

She looked at him and said, "About . . . that night . . ."

"Don't feel foolish."

"I was too dumb to just enjoy it."

He grinned at her and said, "It was my impression that you did enjoy it."

"Well . . . I did, but after I just . . . sort of felt guilty about it . . ."

"About enjoying it?"

She nodded.

"Terry—"

"Never mind, Clint," she said. "It's not important."

"What about the sheep?"

She shrugged and said, "I'm going to ride out to the Lords' ranch and talk to Mrs. Lord later. Maybe she'll be more cooperative than her husband was. I only need a few more days."

"I hope it works out."

"It will," she said. "Thanks to you."

"And to you," Clint said. "You saved my life when you killed Sam Pace."

"Well," she said, "I can't pay you, so I had to do something."

"You did that," he said. He took a step toward her and kissed her cheek. "Say good-bye to Henry John and Margarite for me, will you?"

"I will."

He mounted Duke and looked down at her.

"You going to stay in the sheep business?"

She grinned and said, "Maybe I'll try something else after this."

"Good thinking . . ."

Clint rode back into town and stopped at the sheriff's office.

"What do you want?" Haywood asked defensively, as Clint entered.

"I just wanted to let you know that I'll be stopping at the first town I come to, Sheriff," Clint said. "I'm going to do my best to get some federal law in here. I think that by the time they get here you'd be wise to get out of office. Understand?"

Grudgingly, Haywood said, "I was planning on going back to bein' a blacksmith, anyways."

"Good," Clint said. "Do it in another town."

As Clint left the sheriff's office he looked up at the boarded-up window of Tom Lord's office. He wanted to see Lord's secretary, Kelly Harlowe again, but it wouldn't make much sense to go there now. If she was even up there.

He crossed the street and walked to Randi Travis's office.

When Randi opened the door he asked, "Didn't catch you with a patient, did I?"

"No," she said. "Come in."

He entered and she closed the door.

"Are you leaving?"

"Yes," he said. "This is my last stop. I wanted to thank you."

"For what?"

"Yesterday," he said. "You saved my life when you killed Sam Pace."

She shrugged and said, "It was a lucky shot. I hadn't fired that rifle in a long time."

"Well, I'm glad you were lucky."

"Did you ever find out who killed Lord?"

"No," he said. "And all of the men have left town, already. My guess is that one of them was hired to do a little extra job."

"By who?"

"Maybe Sam Pace," Clint said. "Maybe he and Lord's wife were lovers."

Randi laughed.

"What's so funny?"

"Have you ever seen Olivia Lord?"

"No."

"She was once a handsome woman, and still thinks that she is, but . . ." Randi trailed off and shook her head.

"Well, maybe Pace was in it for the money."

"Maybe. We certainly can't say the same thing about you. You didn't get paid a cent for risking your neck."

Clint shrugged. He didn't want to get into another discussion about why he poked his nose into other people's business.

"Well," he said, "I'd better be going."

She moved close to him and kissed him, sliding her arms around his waist.

"Be back this way?" she asked.

"Never can tell."

"Sure," she said.

" 'Bye," Clint said.

"I'd tell you to keep your nose out of other people's business," she said, "but that wouldn't do much good, so just be careful."

As Clint Adams left she folded her arms and shook her head. The only thing she wished she knew for sure was which shot had killed Sam Pace, hers or Terry Haslett's.

It didn't much matter, though, did it?

Clint left the office and mounted Duke. As he guided the big gelding onto the main street he saw the stage preparing to leave. One of the passengers was that beautiful red-haired woman. Before boarding the stage she looked over at him and smiled. He touched the brim of his hat in reply.

Clint watched the stage leave, noted the direction it was taking, and then rode to the livery to collect his rig.

Watch for

THE DEADLY DERRINGER

121st novel in the exciting GUNSMITH series
from Jove

Coming in January!

If you enjoyed this book, subscribe now and get...

TWO FREE

A $7.00 VALUE–

If you would like to read more of the very best, most exciting, adventurous, action-packed Westerns being published today, you'll want to subscribe to True Value's Western Home Subscription Service.

Each month the editors of True Value will select the 6 very best Westerns from America's leading publishers for special readers like you. You'll be able to preview these new titles as soon as they are published, *FREE* for ten days with no obligation!

TWO FREE BOOKS

When you subscribe, we'll send you your first month's shipment of the newest and best 6 Westerns for you to preview. With your first shipment, two of these books will be yours as our introductory gift to you absolutely *FREE* (a $7.00 value), regardless of what you decide to do. If

you like them, as much as we think you will, keep all six books but pay for just 4 at the low subscriber rate of just $2.75 each. If you decide to return them, keep 2 of the titles as our gift. No obligation.

Special Subscriber Savings

When you become a True Value subscriber you'll save money several ways. First, all regular monthly selections will be billed at the low subscriber price of just $2.75 each. That's at least a savings of $4.50 each month below the publishers price. Second, there is never any shipping handling or other hidden charges—*Free home delivery*. What's more there is no minimum number of books you must buy, you may return any selection for full credit and you can cancel your subscription at any time. A TRUE VALUE!

J.R. ROBERTS
THE
GUNSMITH

___THE GUNSMITH #105: HELLDORADO	0-515-10403-5/$2.95
___THE GUNSMITH #106: THE HANGING JUDGE	0-515-10428-0/$2.95
___THE GUNSMITH #107: THE BOUNTY HUNTER	0-515-10447-7/$2.95
___THE GUNSMITH #108: TOMBSTONE AT LITTLE HORN	0-515-10474-4/$2.95
___THE GUNSMITH #109: KILLER'S RACE	0-515-10496-5/$2.95
___THE GUNSMITH #110: WYOMING RANGE WAR	0-515-10514-7/$2.95
___THE GUNSMITH #111: GRAND CANYON GOLD	0-515-10528-7/$2.95
___THE GUNSMITH #112: GUNS DON'T ARGUE	0-515-10548-1/$2.95
___THE GUNSMITH #113: ST. LOUIS SHOWDOWN	0-515-10572-4/$2.95
___THE GUNSMITH #114: FRONTIER JUSTICE	0-515-10599-6/$2.95
___THE GUNSMITH #115: GAME OF DEATH	0-515-10615-1/$3.50
___THE GUNSMITH #116: THE OREGON STRANGLER	0-515-10651-8/$3.50
___THE GUNSMITH #117: BLOOD BROTHERS	0-515-10671-2/$3.50
___THE GUNSMITH #118: SCARLET FURY	0-515-10691-7/$3.50
___THE GUNSMITH #119: ARIZONA AMBUSH	0-515-10710-7/$3.50
___THE GUNSMITH #120: THE VENGEANCE TRAIL	0-515-10735-2/$3.50